RETURN TO YOUR WORLD

ANJ CAIRNS

Copper Rose Publishing

ISBN: 978-1-9997944-2-2

Disclaimer

This is a work of fiction. Names, characters, places and incidents are either the products of the author's imagination or are used fictitiously, and any resemblance to actual persons, living or dead is entirely coincidental. Certain businesses and organisations are mentioned, but the stories played out in them are wholly imaginary.

*For my tribe - because the most unstoppable smiles
come from unstoppable friends.*

ONE

London 1971

AFTER SIXTEEN HOURS OF LABOUR, Maud Miller gave birth to a boy later to be named John after no one in particular. He appeared in the world through natural child birthing methods in the stark, clinical labour room of the City of London Maternity Hospital. The child arrived with a plume of black feathery newborn hair and showed no resemblance his father or mother. But this had no impact on Maud, as she held his blanketed form to her skin, grinning at the wonder and miracle of human life. She had made a baby.

Birth of this kind wasn't something she would recommend to anyone. It failed to resemble the descriptions Maud read in the books borrowed from her local library. And she realised now that the other wives she knew had limited their tales of the pain, endurance and loneliness of bringing a child into the world for fear of frightening her. Maud's husband Ron had been barred from the delivery room, his pending fatherhood not seen as a reason to watch the miracle of childbirth. Although his nervous chitchat about work and what he was going to eat for dinner while Maud and his son were in the hospital was annoying, she missed his presence by her side as she pushed, panted, and screamed her way to becoming a mother.

Maud and baby John remained in the hospital for four days, in the maternity ward with other new mothers, some of whom she knew from the antenatal classes offered by the National Childbirth Trust. During her pregnancy, she had attempted to get Ron to accompany her to the sessions, but he had found excuses, saying he was too busy to take an hour away from work each week. Maud went to the first session alone and endured the sideways stares of the couples in the room. Maud couldn't stop thinking her antenatal companions suspected her to be a single mother who had conceived her child in a sinful unmarried act. It was a stain she couldn't rub off at night with a flannel and a bar of Pears soap in the bathtub. It tainted the experience. In subsequent weeks, Maud made sure to mention her husband in conversation, and the social chatter began to relax as the attendees forged bonds based on their shared predicament.

Despite the limitations of formal pre-birth preparation and a lack of experience of parenting, Maud surprised herself by taking to motherhood as if she had been doing it for many lifetimes. John's conception had been unexpected, and at the age of thirty-three, the medical profession tagged her pregnancy as geriatric. In the hospital and at her childbirth classes, all the women were younger than her, sporting fresh, youthful enthusiasm and skin to match. The age difference reminded Maud she would never experience things with the eyes of the young, but she had more knowledge to apply to the essential life task of being a mother than her peers.

The process of bonding with her tiny male offspring brought her a joy she had never imagined possible and arrested her sense of not being like everyone else. For the first time since she arrived in London, Maud had a purpose and a meaningful role. She was a mum.

After being discharged from the ward, Maud and John were returned to the comfort of their small two-bedroom terrace house in Tufnell Park by Ron who fussed over Maud and the baby throughout the short taxi journey. His enthusiasm waned come night time when Maud arose to feed and soothe the cries from the infant, and in the days following their homecoming, she felt closer to her child and disconnected from her husband.

Swaddled in a hand-knitted blue blanket, John began to cry. A soft whimper at first, building to an ear-drum bursting yell no adult could reproduce.

"Hello, precious. You're awake again, are you?" Maud rubbed his tummy through the cover before dipping down to the cot and scooping him up into a supported position in her arms. "Look at you, all gorgeous. Are you hungry? Mummy will make you up a bottle." Reluctant to put the baby down, Maud struggled one-handed to heat the milk on the stove. "Shush now, the bottle's nearly done." John continued to wail as she tested the temperature of the milk by squeezing some on her wrist. "Okay, precious, time for food."

The pair settled down in a comfortable spot on a kitchen chair. Outside, the heat of the August sun was fading into the early evening lull, and as she put the half-drunk bottle of formula down on the floor next to them, both mother and child fell into a contented doze.

"Evening."

The intruding male voice woke Maud and set John off on another session of baby-pitched wailing.

"Hello, love. we lost track of time."

"How's my little man?" Ron loosened his tie and held out his hands. Maud passed John over to him.

"Careful. Remember to support his neck." She fussed with John's baby blanket before stepping away.

"You don't have to keep telling me. Besides, I'm at the office all day, dealing with idiots and fending off strikes by the blasted miners. When I get home, I want to relax and spend time with my boy. You've got all day to sleep in a chair with him."

Maud boiled. What did he know about her life? Ron never asked about how she coped in the long hours when he worked in Central London. He didn't understand how exhausting it was to be so in love with a tiny being that you couldn't take your eyes off for fear of missing some threat; a high temperature, hunger, a filled nappy. She said nothing.

"What's for dinner?" asked Ron.

"Corned beef hash. It'll be ready in a bit. Why don't you take John through to the lounge and watch the news and 'London This Week'? I'll shout you when the food is done."

Her tall, slightly overweight husband stood up and kissed her on the cheek.

"Alright, love. Can we have beans with it?"

"Of course. Oh, are the miners really going to strike?" she asked as he made his way out of the kitchen.

Ron shrugged. "They keep talking about it. Doubt anything will happen though."

Maud set about making the dinner, imagining a day when food would involve more flavour, less work and a machine could do the washing up.

TWO

The Core

____

DURING HER TIME living as a human female with the Townsends and Trevor in North London, Sketch had made every effort to fix the computer in which her world, the Core resided. While the machine was inoperable, she had been stuck in the capital city, in a physical body with a weight which tethered her to the human sphere. Though surrounded by kind friends and people she considered to be her adopted family, Sketch had yearned to get back to the Core and resume her previous existence as a computer energy.

Sketch's eventual return from the human world was not the illustrious event she'd imagined it would be, and the ways of the Core left her homesick and confused. The absence of colour in the Core perturbed Sketch who had become accustomed to the vast spectrum of shades and pigments which humans could see. She found the conformity of each day in the Core mundane and the lack of personality demonstrated by her fellow energies drained her.

She surveyed her surrounds. The Core functioned in monochrome, with energies communicating through pulses. Their state of being was illustrated by surges of light and darkness; highs indicated by spinning and twirling to produce a light show not dissimilar to a firework display but without the colours. Vibrancy equalled bright white light and success the same. Darkness, in contrast, represented discontent and failure. During Sketch's previous time in the Core, vibrancy was encouraged, sought after, demonstrating an energetic pride in serving the human users of the machine. Now, the atmosphere had metamorphosed. The status quo dictated that each energy should strive to follow its routine, moderate their displays of light, constrain their auras to a neutral level. Sketch recalled her initial communication with the One on her return to the Core. Her confusion at being met by unfamiliar energies had sent her aura into free-fall. Sparks flew at random, beams of light and dark pushed out from her being, all dimming when the One barked a pulse in her direction.

"Halt your aura deviations. Such displays will not be tolerated under my regime."

"Sorry, where is the One? I mean the other the One?" pulsed Sketch, attempting to control her aura flow.

"Gone. It exhibited insufficient regulation resulting in a catastrophic breakdown of the functions of the Core. Not sending you for recycling following your ill-conceived actions proved to be the final mistake in a series of bad decisions."

"Gone where?" Sketch asked, her other question about whether or not he planned to terminate her existence as a computer energy left untransmitted.

"Transformed." The One's tone fluctuated between one of boredom and one of irritation.

"Into what?"

"Enough of your questions. It is enough for you to be aware that it and its charges have gone and won't be returning."

"What...what about me?"

"Enough of your questions. Questions will not be tolerated. You've been assigned a work station and task. Given your history of failure, your duties are of a level where you can bring no harm to humans. Is this acceptable?"

In an effort not to become engulfed in a darkening of her aura, Sketch indicated the affirmative and had been dispatched by the One to a work station to perform basic duties.

Sketch quivered at the meanness inherent in the One's pulses. Its predecessor seemed tame in comparison, though at the time Sketch had quivered before her too. She wondered if her time with humans had resulted in her abandoning her kind, her ways of thinking and behaving, but instinct told her otherwise. The One reminded her of Winston, the Head of the Library Service in the cross-borough council of Northgate. He ruled his employees with a selfish lack of logic and refused to give any thought to what local people wanted, resulting in the planned closure of the Northgate library. The main difference between the One and Winston was that for the most part, people ignored the ineffectual manager, but the energies of the Core conformed without question to the commands of the One.

Her allocated task was simple. She acted as a third level back up to the display adjustment function on the computer's monitor. As a job, it ranked amongst the most boring an energy could be assigned. With older desktop machines, human users tended not to adjust the settings, and the probability of the two energies before her failing to complete their task in the rare event of a human selecting this option fell outside of a statistical chance. She realised it wasn't a job function at all. More a punishment to show her and her fellow energies how little importance should be attached to her time in the human realm.

"Hello," pulsed Sketch to display adjuster energies number one and two. At least some conversation would go some way to passing the time. Both ignored her. They remained positioned ready to act, and their auras were blank and unwavering. Sketch deliberated what they would do if she began to spark out lights. The idea was tempting, but she decided now was not the time for dramatic displays.

"My name is Sketch. What's yours?" Again, her pulses met with silence. "Well, I have to call you something, and it would be rude to name you display adjuster one and two, so I will call you Cleo and Charmaine." *Naming something makes it real,* thought Sketch. *Perhaps they will come to trust me in time.*

She decided to do what she could to convince the One she was unproblematic. Her display adjuster backup role ensured she remained error-free; errors having been the reason for her mandatory time spent learning what life is like for human users. Her thoughts corkscrewed around in a fashion her aura wasn't permitted to, then settled as she considered her options. There were three: One, remain in the Core, adhere to this unfamiliar regime and live the existence planned for her. Two, find a way of bringing the kindness, love and pride of the earlier version of the computer back to the Core. Or three, discover a way back to the human world, to her friends, Inco and the other energies she hoped had also transformed into people. The first option held no sway with her having learned too much from humanity to reside in a world without beauty and compassion. However, as yet she couldn't decide which of the latter options was for the best. For now, she held off from making a decision. In the meantime, she must find a way to get to the human user viewing platform, an area of the computer she no longer had access to. There she could check her human friends and Inco were okay and reassure them her transformation had been a success.

THREE

London 2014

____

NOT FOR THE first time that week, Matt trudged up the ten sets of stairs to Trevor's fifth floor flat, once again cursing the building's lack of lift. The purple doorway to the flats nestled between two retail outlets and the levels above rested above a new cafe patronised in the main by local mothers, fathers and their small children. Trevor lived too far up for the aroma of premium coffee to waft up to his flat, and Matt wished the coffee was at the top, not the bottom. That way it would justify the effort it took to get up there. Each occasion he did the climb he set off believing he was fit and energetic, but by the time he got to Trevor's door his body would give in to the need to puff and pant. He wondered if this is what people with asthma went through and if he should ask his doctor for an inhaler, just in case.

"Matt, I'll have to be getting you a key at this rate," said Trevor opening the door and handing the gasping teenager a glass of water.

"Not a bad idea, mate."

"You here to help with the library stuff?" Trevor said, his face deadpan. Matt stared back. He wasn't sure what Trevor was on about. Every day, he turned up to see Sketch, to try to communicate

9

to her from the outside of the computer. He couldn't give a frick about the library and the crazy plan to take it over and run it by themselves. The only thing that interested him was getting Sketch back.

"I'm joking, young 'un." Trevor gestured towards the computer, positioned on top of the small round kitchen table behind the sofa as if a feature piece of the room. The power remained connected twenty-four hours a day, for fear that turning it off would result in it crashing again; this time forever.

"I'm off for a shower, so I'll leave you to it. Say hello from me," said Trevor.

Matt grabbed a chair and plonked himself down opposite the screen.

"'Hello, Sketch." He paused, hoping for some sort of sign that she could hear him and that he wasn't talking to the desktop running an ancient version of Windows.

"How have you been? Must be weird to be back in there, or maybe being in the computer is like coming home for you. I went around to Dominic's last night. Like I said I would. He's the most techie geek I know. He's thinking about how we can get you back. Back to us, where you belong." Matt yawned, stretching up to ruffle his hair with one hand.

"Other than that, not much is happening. Got an essay to do for school. Not that my grades matter now I've pulled my UCAS application."

Both his mum Jackie and Ashling had been relieved when he did a U-turn on going to university in the autumn. He had let them believe he'd done it because of Sammy, the son he had with Ashling, but the real reason was Sketch. He couldn't risk leaving her, alone inside a computer without any contact with the outside world. Not when it was his fault, she was there in the first place. If he'd told her how he felt about her instead of chickening out and walking away, she would be here now making everyone smile.

"Now I'm not going to uni, mum and dad are on at me about looking for a job. Exams will be over soon, and everything's over. No more school, no summer holidays, just selling my soul for money. And it would all be okay if you were here. I miss you."

His mind tried to picture Sketch in human form, her spiky blonde hair, taller than average height and that smile. The contagious smile which accompanied her gregarious optimism. His mind couldn't hold the image in place, but he smiled all the same.

A buzzing emerged from the intercom beside the front door. Matt hesitated. Was it okay to answer someone else's door when they were in the shower? He decided to leave it and return to his conversation with Sketch. However, the caller persisted in ringing the bell on the ground floor, so Matt strolled across the open plan living space and picked up the receiver.

"Hello."

"Trevor? It's Michael. I'm here to look at the computer like we agreed."

Oh, thought Matt, divided in his option about Michael. On the one hand, the man understood more about how computers operated than anyone else because he had been a computer energy too. But, on the other hand, as an energy in the Core Michael had lived with Sketch, understood her, loved her.

"Err hi, Matt here. Trevor's in the shower."

"Can you buzz me in? He's expecting me."

Matt listened to the static of the intercom.

"Matt? Are you there? The door's not open," said Michael.

"Yeh, sorry. Come up." He pressed the enter button to release the exterior door and replaced the receiver in its cradle.

It pleased Matt that Michael also arrived at the top of the stairs panting and puffing. And because beads of sweat formed in the space where the older man's hair had receded. The two stood on either side of the sofa, not speaking and avoiding making eye contact with each other.

Michael nodded at the computer. "Have you been talking to her?"

"Yeh, are you certain she can hear us?"

"I can't think why not. The Core is designed, so its energies are required to observe human users, to learn about their IT habits and their interests, to respond quickly when one of you wants to watch a video on YouTube, search the internet for historical facts or showcase your lives on social media."

"Our lives? Aren't you one of us now?"

Michael shrugged. "I suppose after all this time I am, but the Core is my last remembered home, and the life of an energy without physical form is unparalleled in the human realm."

Matt gritted his teeth. "And you think you can do something to bring Sketch back?"

"I can try, but it depends on whether or not she wants to return. Don't gurn at me. I'm being honest with you. Telling it like it is."

"But why wouldn't she want to return? Everything and everyone Sketch loves is here in North London."

"But London isn't her world. You can't begin to imagine how lonely it is to live here knowing there is so much more to existence."

"And would you go back if you had the choice?"

Michael walked over to the computer and ran his fingers over its casing. "No, it has its attractions, it will always be where I existed, but home is here with Clare."

FOUR

London 1971

———————————————

IT DIDN'T TAKE Maud long to discover that leaving the house with a small baby in tow required a level of effort and preparation that almost rendered the journey worthless. In addition to packing up terry towelling nappies, rash cream, bottles of formula ready for heating, wipes, changes of clothes and toys, she worried about forgetting she had a child, that something awful would happen to him on the high street or that at any moment she would give into sleep, sit down on the pavement and cry herself to sleep. Despite this, she wrapped up three-month-old John in a miniature winter outfit and bundled him under a pile of blankets, a blue knitted bonnet covering his head.

They were headed to the coffee morning at the local church hall where Maud had arranged to meet her friend Beverley for drinks and chit chat. The pair had met in the maternity ward and, enjoying each other's company, stayed in touch on their respective returns home.

Maud shivered at the chill breath of the wind as it whipped and slapped at her face. She wondered if the winter would last forever and why it was she'd ended up on this side of the hemisphere and not in sunnier climes. As she wandered through the streets of

Kentish Town, the sights of local characters and shops gave her a familiar sense of belonging.

The church coffee morning was one of the few places she was able to meet with other people with little children. Beverley had been in the bed next to her when she gave birth to John. Though younger than Maud, the woman had an amiable disposition and struggled with her life in London. This much they had in common. Beverley and her husband Clifford had recently arrived in the UK, enticed away from the Caribbean by the promise of jobs, housing and a more attractive future for them and their children. A perfect advert for an idyllic future. Loneliness had not been included in the package but loomed larger than life for Beverley. Being stuck at home with a tiny baby intensified this loneliness for both Maud and Beverley.

Maud was far from religious and didn't attend services at the church, but she was happy to have a local space where she could chat over the struggles of motherhood, its joys and whether or not her child was doing as it should do for his age. Beverly was more of a churchgoer, the communal coming together to worship reminded her of home, despite the Church of England services being different in tone and style to those she was used to.

If Maud disliked the cold, Beverley hated it with a vengeance. She layered on clothing wherever possible, with tights and socks under jeans accompanied on top by vests, tops and jumpers, finished with a not quite thick enough black coat, a bobble hat, scarf and gloves. The bright red of Beverley's knitted winter warmers attracted Maud's eye as she turned the corner to the path which led to the church hall. She waved, smiled and pushed on up the hill to greet her friend.

"Hello, hello," Maud said. "Let's get inside out of this bitter wind."

"Oh, you're a woman after my own heart, Maud. I've a chill in my bones I fear will never leave." The pair pushed through the heavy door and navigated their way between the other prams, rearranging wheels and carriages until they managed to park up their baby vehicles.

"Hello, ladies. Grab yourselves a cup of tea or coffee and some biscuits. Nothing homemade today, I'm afraid, but there are some custard creams and bourbons in the tin. Be quick, we're about to start with some singing." The enunciated words hailed from a mouth of a well-meaning, middle-class woman, dressed in flared cord trousers and a tight-fitting polo neck jumper, and sporting long flowing brown hair parted down the midline of her head. "Today is nursery rhyme time," she said, directing her words towards Beverley. "Don't worry if you don't know the songs. You'll soon get the hang of it."

Maud caught Beverley's eye and sent her a smile encoded with a message intended to say, 'Ignore her."

"They have nursery rhymes back home, you know. Maybe I can teach the group some new ones."

"That's an excellent idea, isn't it, Jenny?" added Maud, a twinkle beginning to spread from her eyes to the corners of her mouth. Jenny muttered her agreement and left them to pour over-brewed tea into brown and orange mugs.

"Don't mind her," said Maud. "She's trying to do the right thing, say the right things, but she's forgotten you're just another human being."

"Things, well, things have been hard, Maud. Ever since we arrived here, people have stared at us in the street, called us all kinds of names. As hurtful as it is, and it's as hurtful as the English winter, people like Jenny are worse. They think they see beyond our dark skin and foreign accents but still talk to us as if we haven't a brain cell between us. Britain doesn't feel like the home it promised to be."

Maud shuddered on the inside. Beverley's words were her opinion but also, as Maud saw it, typical of the time and the experience of decades of immigrants who arrived in the UK hoping for a glorious life. She shuddered knowing that while this culture of racism would change in the future, it would never be eradicated. Without adequate words to reassure her friend, Maud resorted to a gentle smile and squeezing Beverley's hand.

"Let's get the kiddies settled," she said. "I'm sure Jenny is raring to go with a rendition of 'Ten Green Bottles' or 'Mary, Mary'."

Beverley managed to bring back her smile and aimed it at Maud. "And I'm going to teach everyone, 'Mosquito one, mosquito two'."

It struck Maud that people would find their lives easier to live if kindness had a more significant place in the day to day than the suspicion which led to ignorant comments and assumptions such as the ones Jenny had made about Beverley and her life. She winced to think about what they would say if they knew the truth about her history.

FIVE

The Core

—————————

DESPITE BEHAVING in the way which was expected of her, showing diligence, compliance and obedience to the rules, Sketch didn't sense that she was any more trusted or accepted. Instead, she felt as if she were little more than an inconsequential part of a massive unstoppable machine. A screw left over after of hours of constructing flatpack furniture. As a newcomer to this revitalised, unfamiliar version of the Core, she played no vital role in its continued existence, and she had no idea how to change this.

Multiple work sessions lapsed, but still, no opportunity for Sketch to transfer to a more challenging role had appeared. Nor had she discovered a way to travel from her work station to the human viewing platform. Her aura grew darker as she collapsed under the weight of her thinking.

In the darkness and stillness of the human night, a time little activity happened with the computer, except on a couple of occasions when Trevor arrived home in the wee hours and stabbed at the keyboard, Sketch reached her lowest. Her belief in hope, goodness and there always being a way to change things risked being extinguished. Another shift ended. She pulsed leaving greetings with Cleo and Charmaine who behaved as they ever did, ignoring her pulses. They stayed motionless in standby mode, not appearing to listen or care about Sketch's attempts to communicate with them or what she did during the downtime between shifts.

No, I won't be this person, she thought. *But how can I change anything when I'm trapped and alone?* Her thinking whirled and twisted, leading to dead ends in complex mazes and unscalable towers but no plan of action. While she bounced thoughts around her personal echo chamber, a familiar voice broke through pulsing to her.

"Nothing's impossible, Sketch. Difficult maybe but not impossible. Like they say, 'If life gives you lemons, make lemonade.'"

"Why would you add sugar to lemons? You'll lose the goodness of the fruit," said Sketch before wondering who was communicating with her. "Who is this?"

Sketch received no reply. She recognised the voice but not who it belonged to or where it came from. It wasn't unusual for messages in the form of pulses to traverse the expanse of the Core; however, this voice appeared disconnected to the usual channels vibrations would travel.

Despite not having a clue why the voice was talking to her about lemons, it proved a welcome distraction from the day to day drudge of her life. At the very least, someone had chosen to communicate with her, beyond checking she was complying with the strict dictates of the Core's internal environment.

Lemons were extraordinary, Sketch pulsed to herself, bringing up a waxy image of the rounded shape, its pimpled skin and the acidic yet refreshing tang of juice emerging from the inside of the fruit when a knife sliced it into equal sized wedges. Her experience of lemons was restricted to the healthy foodstuffs Jackie had worked hard to encourage her to eat. Lemons did, however, cause her to recall a night out with Begw and Trevor in the Pineapple pub, where Kentish Town bumps up against Tufnell Park. There, a gin and tonic always came accompanied by a segment of lemon. *And why?* she thought. *Why would the voice be communicating about lemons when lemons didn't exist in the matrix of the Core?*

For the first time since returning to the Core and discovering its dystopian transformation, Sketch found herself lightening and her aura lifting from a state of grey nothingness.

A buzzer vibrated, signalling the beginning of the next shift. The breaks between work periods were getting shorter. Sketch's aura plummeted as she gravitated back to her station awaiting the inspirational talk by the One which now preceded any session.

"Energies of the Core. You have chosen to serve the humans. We are servants to their needs and wants. When you perform your actions, they smile, function and grow. When you fail, the humans falter. They reach for aggression and spread their disharmony and discord to those in their spheres. The humans are our masters. Fail them at your peril for they and they alone have the power to send you for recycling - the ultimate of punishments."

Sketch spun with fury inside. The pulses of the One were lies. Nothing but a collection of made up ideas. Words twisted and forged to make everyone afraid. The humans weren't aware their computers were run by energies and the odd mention of gremlins within causing problems was put down to their lack of understanding of the technology they believed their scientists had invented. Perhaps the One wasn't aware of the truth. *Maybe the One had received incomplete data or missed elements of basic training,* thought Sketch. *Yes, that must be it.* But even if this proved to be the reason, the One managed the Core in a manner she deemed to be inappropriate. In a way which removed joy and replaced it with tyranny. Sketch attempted to rationalise the reasons for this but couldn't come up with anything other than a vague theory that the One's actions had to be for the good of the Core.

If the One had been mistaken or misled about the humans, Sketch could help the One to understand the truth and make it easier for them to rule in a way which benefitted both those in the human world and the inhabitants of the Core. With a surge of determination, Sketch left her allotted space as the shift began, embracing the glow she experienced in coming up with this master plan, and projected her being towards the realm of the One.

SIX

London 2014

MICHAEL AND CLARE were coming to terms with a new reality. One where Michael had an alternative name and a former life, and one where human scientific knowledge appeared laughable in the face of a world where energies from a defective computer were dispersed in different forms throughout the human world. Although Clare could rationalise it all on a factual level, in a 'this is the sensible, grown-up way' to approach the sudden changes in her life, she struggled to balance this logic with her emotional, gut reaction to the situation. Her life resembled a pane of glass smashed into fragments. The pieces were all there, but even if it were possible to put them back together, the glass would never look or feel the same. If Clare was a fairy tale, she thought she would be Humpty Dumpty.

"We could look at it differently," said Michael. "Have you heard of Kintsugi, the Japanese thing?"

Clare shook her head.

"Kintsugi is the art of putting broken pottery back together. Artists highlight the cracks by filling them with gold. That way it recognises the changes as part of what it is now."

"That's beautiful and kind of wise, but I'm not sure how all the pieces even fit together now."

Michael took her hand in his, pulled her fingers towards him and kissed them. "As long as we're together, we'll find the fit."

Clare wished she could be comforted by the warmth of his words and the reassurance he seemed to want to give her, but she also wanted to ask the unspeakable questions that refused to stop tumbling around in her head. *What about Sketch? How do you feel about Sketch? What if you could go back too? Would you leave me? How can I be enough?*

"Yeh, I guess." She raised a smile hoping it was convincing. She guessed it worked as Michael's face showed no sign of concern. "So, what shall we do today? It's not raining, we're still in the middle of summer, and we live in one of the best cities in the world."

"What about going somewhere new? I've heard things are happening in Tottenham."

"Tottenham? Isn't it a bit scary there?"

Michael stared back at her wide-eyed. "Clare! You are beginning to sound like. Well, I don't know what." They both laughed, sharing a moment of together time which reminded Clare of their lives before the chaos created by the arrival of Sketch. She glowed inside and smiled outside.

"Okay, so what's with Tottenham?"

"Apparently they have the best coffee in the world and a canal."

"Really?"

"Why shouldn't Tottenham have the best coffee in the world?" asked Michael his face reverting to brain scan mode. His head tilted upwards. His lips were whispering as he considered the evidence he located in his memory. She stroked the side of his face. "No reason," she said. "I didn't know they had a canal over that way. Coffee and a walk sounds lovely. Let's do that."

As they gathered keys, phones, money and the other essential accoutrements of modern life, Clare's thoughts wound back to how they came to be living together in London, far from their suburban new town and previous lives. Michael had rung her to say he was moving to London. The call came in the depth of the night. Her mind was confused, in a world of dreams and replying to his announcement, she spoke from her gut instead of from the common-sense approach she applied to her life on a day-to-day basis.

"Don't go."

"What do I have to stay for?" he asked.

"Me, stay for me."

The line went silent. The sort of silence caused by the other person not knowing what to say. The kind of silence brought on by finally admitting to yourself that you have feelings for someone.

"Michael?"

"Clare?"

"Say something. Please say something," she whispered, remembering her husband Steve was snoring upstairs.

"I can't.

"Then I'll come with you."

Every time Clare spoke, she shocked herself with the words that emerged from her mouth. She'd just offered to leave her husband, her job and move away with a man she hadn't even kissed. A man who had years

The wait for Michael's reply messed with time. The gap between her words and his was seconds but seemed like years to Clare. Her mind churned like a mixed load wash. But she knew now Michael was too important to her to lose.

"Yes." His one-word reply had changed everything. That one word transformed her life.

The events that followed became blurred in her memories; telling Steve and her parents about her decision and then packing up the essential bits and pieces of her life. It turned out there were few things she wanted to take with her. This surprised her then, but now the surprises were commonplace. Fear mingled with a sense of exhilaration and an overpowering need to smile when she thought of Michael. She grinned at the memory of their joint smiling. Through the everyday of their lives, they'd sewn a thread of love binding them together. But now they knew Michael wasn't of human origin Clare feared their smiles wouldn't be enough to keep them together.

Michael appeared unperturbed by the change in his understanding of who he was and his place in the world. At least, as it related to their relationship. When it came to Sketch, Clare knew his thoughts were never a long distance from considering how and if to rescue her from the Core. She sighed and then checked Michael hadn't noticed her bad mood. It was better that she gave herself a shake, force herself to be positive and enjoy the day. The world's best coffee or maybe just London's most delicious coffee awaited her and Michael, along with a walk along the canal in the throes of late summer sunshine. Clare tucked her arm around Michael's and kissed him on the cheek. London was the happiest place to be in the sunshine of the summer.

SEVEN

London 1976

MAUD'S early days in London had left her unsatisfied. The city was wondrous; full of rollercoaster rides of potential: things to do, people to meet, experiences to be lived. Yet, despite this, she was filled with an unanticipated hollowness and the dissatisfaction of acute boredom. Then, having a child transformed her. After the painful last push of labour, surrounded by the cries of her baby, oxytocin had flooded Maud with love. As produced this purest emotion, she began to live life and see its beauty. She lightened.

On becoming a mother, the everyday duties of bringing up baby consumed Maud. John proved to be an easy infant, suffering the usual childhood illnesses, cuts and bruises, but one who laughed and smiled more than he cried.

As the bond between mother and child grew, Maud's relationship with Ron deteriorated. They talked less, stopped eating together and turned away from one another at night, an invisible barrier between his body and hers. Ron played with John, bathed him and encouraged him to kick a football around their undersized back garden, but Maud and her husband no longer talked about the big things like politics and love, their conversations turned from caring to functional. Maud suspected Ron saw her only as a mother for his child and nothing else, and in response she dedicated her time and attention to John and his upbringing. But this only furthered the growing distance between husband and wife.

To the eyes and ears of onlookers in the family and their social network, the couple appeared solid. At times, she questioned the choice she made to wed the first man she met who could help her to disguise her true nature. However, Ron had ticked her rigorous criteria for a father of her child. And, she reflected, he had, unbeknown to him, assisted her to stick to her pre-determined path.

When John started at the local infant school, Maud found herself directionless. Hours appeared in her day wanting to be filled with something other than childcare or housework, but she struggled to see what that something was. Part-time jobs open to women with children were scarce, as working needed to fit in the space between the start and finish of the school day. The top options included working in a shop or being a dinner lady. Neither appealed to Maud, but she decided to raise the idea about getting a job with her fellow mothers after dropping off John at the school gates. Her query was met by with raised eyebrows. Her small circle of parent friends didn't understand why she should want to go out to work when her husband earned enough to provide for the whole family. Some, like Beverley, had no choice. For them, work provided food and clothing for their kids and paid the rent. But Maud, while not having problems keeping the electric meter topped up, wanted something more in her life to nourish her starving brain. She needed it if she was going to make it through to the next century.

Without a job, Maud gravitated towards the library to read the day's newspapers after leaving John with his teacher. The building opened in 1967, and provided a quiet sanctuary from the bustle of the North London streets where her family lived. She devoured the news printed in red top rags to more highbrow broadsheets, each bringing their own slant on the complex issues facing people across the world. Delving into books and dipping into journals and newspapers kept her brain alert and prevented her store of information from deteriorating before a time when it would be of use to her. It was there in the library that Maud wrote a letter that wouldn't be delivered until after her death, and recorded her day-to-day experiences in narrow lined spiral-bound notebooks with a view that one day they would be read by someone who might benefit from her ramblings. Her diary of events was illustrated with complex diagrams showing how her activities connected to the more significant events of history as it unfolded. Her scribblings began in the summer of 1976 and stopped in the autumn of 2013 when her life came to an abrupt halt as a bus hit her one morning on the Kentish Town Road as she made her way to the local library via the post office to pick up her pension.

EIGHT

The Core

AS SKETCH APPROACHED the vicinity of the One, she began to question her courage. Like late night ingenious plans pushed away by the morning her nerve abandoned her. Sketch anticipated a negative reaction from the One. How could she a disgraced energy, confront the leadership, question the wisdom and experience of the supreme power? She considered turning back, but her conscience prevented her from doing so.

"It's not all about you, Sketch."

"What about the energies living in fear of humans?"

"Don't be selfish."

"What would your human friends think?"

Oh, why is this so hard? she asked herself.

The decision was whisked from her control as a tremendous surge of vibration took her to the One. She quivered. Compared to the previous incumbent, this the One was terrifying, but life in the human world had given Sketch a grasp of fear and how it can hold you back. She wasn't about to become paralysed by it.

"Who permitted you to approach me unbeckoned?" The One dispensed with attempts to disguise his disregard for Sketch.

"I desire to help you."

"Help me? You? How in the Core do you imagine you might do this? Why do you dare to imagine? It is a human characteristic you should have disposed of on your exit from their realm."

Sketch paused before replying, considering which of the four questions to answer first. "I hold knowledge of the humans. They don't have the power to send us for recycling. They don't even know we exist."

The space around them grew murky. The type of dark where monsters lurk, where shadows and nightmares are formed. Then as if someone flicked a switch, light with the clarity of sunlight flooded the space between them.

"You have been brainwashed by those you met in the exterior. We can help you return to the fold; to be the energy you were destined to be. Stay with us, Sketch. Tell me all you know, and we will enhance your status."

Sketch, not suspicious by nature, had in recent months become adept at reading the subtle changes both humans and energies display in their behaviour. The One's transformed demeanour appeared anything but subtle. She measured her options against each other. By refusing the One's request Sketch risked being terminated. This would be worse than recycling to a different form. It would bring about the end of her essence. A permanent death. But, if she agreed to his terms, there was a chance of making things better, bringing things back to how they were supposed to be.

"Let us help you. Let us nourish you, Sketch. You can offer much to the Core if you allow yourself to be assisted."

She began to realize how it was other energies in the Core went along with the One. His aura exuded a hypnotizing charm, his pulses smooth, comforting. The light surrounding the One was different from any she had seen before in her existence as a computer energy or as a human. His entity presented her with a mesmerizing puzzle. She kept checking herself, reminding herself why she was there. The One presented as a tyrant, a liar and a manipulator and she couldn't be drawn into falling for his lies. However, it was within her power to pretend.

"Well," she said. "I suppose there are some things I can help you with too. If you are interested, I'm sure you are still much more informed than me. "

Unsure the One believed her, Sketch continued to communicate in a style she hoped would convince him by appealing to his ego.

"It would be a privilege to work for you," she pulsed. "Someone so admired and powerful within the Core."

"Silence. I've absorbed your request. There is validity in your reasoning, and we will recondition you through our re-education programme. This is a notable consideration I would not extend to all, but you may be of benefit as we continue to build and restructure."

"I appreciate you giving me this chance," said Sketch. "What happens next?"

"Go back to your position. Undertake your duties until you are summoned. And Sketch."

"Yes?"

"There will be no more talk that undermines the supremacy of the humans. Do you comprehend?"

"I do."

The One dismissed Sketch, and as instructed she gravitated back in the direction of her work station, resisting the urge to demonstrate her feelings through the brightness of her aura. As she approached her position, prepared for the monotonous tasks in front of her, a voice, the same voice that had spoken to her before boomed out.

"Now is the time for you to be enlightened."

She twisted around, checking her fellow energies for their reactions, but they appeared oblivious to the pulses which Sketch could hear.

"Who are you? How are you doing this?" she said, keeping her vibrations as low as possible so as not to attract suspicion.

"I am part of a movement, a surge of energies who resist the oppression of the One. We are part of the Resistance."

Sketch paused to evaluate the strange words. The idea of a resistance was alien to her. She had no knowledge of the existence, then or in the past, of a resistance. Could this be a test set by the One to trick her?

"You haven't explained how no one else but me can interpret your pulses."

"Because of the Algorithm. We can manipulate who has access to certain information. It is hard to do and takes much reserve of lightness, but it was necessary to reach you without the One becoming aware."

"How do I know I can trust you? You are unknown to me."

"Oh, but you are still a young un after all, despite your adventures in the human world."

"But? Are you?" Sketch stumbled to catch up with her thoughts as she began to realise which of the energies the voice belonged to.

"Yes, young un. I am Virder."

NINE

London 2014

THE DAILY EXCHANGES of conversation between Begw and Trevor remained terse, despite a brief truce when Sketch disappeared back into the Townsend's ageing computer. Shock transcended everything happening in their lives at the time, but now Trevor was back to responding to Begw with polite phrases and one-word answers of the type used with an unpopular boss. Begw was at a loss to understand what had brought on his perplexing behaviour. They had worked together for years with general, gentle banter as the norm and Trevor's coldness didn't make sense. As she opened up the library for another day of lending books, chatting to borrowers and browsers and dealing with the stupid bureaucracy which accompanies publicly funded services, Begw hoped today would be different. *Imagine if someone decided there'd be no more paperwork or threats of closure to the library and she could spend the day talking to the myriad of people who came through the glass sliding doors,* she thought before sighing. She flicked her super-straight fringe into place and put the kettle on. Making a panad, the word for a cuppa in North Wales, was something she usually delegated to Trevor, but their frosty impasse called for drastic measures on the hot beverage front.

As she waited for her colleague to arrive, Begw flipped to the messaging app on her phone. It was approaching midnight in Sydney, but she hoped Deborah would still be awake. The time difference made it impractical to call and tough to have decent conversations. One was always saying goodnight when the other was starting the day. She pinged off a message instead.

- Night you. If you're working from home tomorrow, let's Skype. I'll stay up. We should make some decisions.

She waited and flashed a grin at her phone as a reply materialised on the screen. Her thoughts flipped to focus on her memories of Sketch. There must be energies like her inside the smartphone. "Morning, phone people," she said before returning her attention to the message, the main reason she was smiling.

- Hey you. Morning. Yes, I'll be working from bed in my pjs. ;-) Now, go share books with the people of London. X

Begw stuffed her phone into her pocket as the door creaked open.

"Morning," said Trevor, without catching her eye as he shuffled into the staffroom at the back of the library.

"Hi, Trevor. I've made you a coffee." Begw shoved a cup of hot water, instant coffee and the smallest amount of milk possible. It was how she liked it, so she figured it would be good enough for Trevor as well.

"Errrr, no thanks. I'm off milky drinks this month."

Well, that's a slap in the face, Begw thought. It gave her pause to consider if she should tell him about her decision. That way, he might understand.

"Fancy going to The Pineapple tonight?" she asked.

"I think I'm busy."

She stopped herself from responding with her automatic response to the busy excuse - 'busy watching paint dry'. Trevor didn't look like he was in the mood for jokes; even funny ones. "Just one then? I'm buying, and I've something I want to talk to you about."

Trevor raised an eyebrow. "Talk to me about what?"

"I'll tell you later. It'll take too long to explain now, and we're due to open up in five minutes."

"Oh, go on then. They've a new beer in I want to check out. Popped up on my Beer about Town app this morning, so I'll come for one. As long as you pay that is."

Begw nodded. The duo fell back into silence and proceeded to do an awkward dance to get past one another until Trevor came to a halt, immobile on the spot and let Begw exit to the library.

With her gone, he grabbed a carton of milk from the fridge and poured a dollop of it into the cup of coffee on the counter. He gulped it down, enjoying the power of the warm liquid and its caffeine content perk to him up. Would have been a waste to pour it down the sink, he told himself.

With Begw intent on talking, tonight might be the perfect time for him to confront her about her involvement with the plans to close the library? Either that or he could get her drunk with a stream of double gin and tonics and hope she revealed some vital information he could use in his attempts to get funding to save the library. Nah, even if he was annoyed and frustrated with her, he couldn't do that. He was going to have to meet her head-on with the truth.

He groaned. Today was story time which reminded him of Sketch. She'd been so good with the little snot-filled creatures who wriggled and giggled and cried during each session. And he missed her. He decided to read that day's stories and rhymes as if she was whispering in his ear telling him what Sketch would do or say.

TEN

London 1978

MAUD CHEWED on the plastic end of her biro. It was one of her small but satisfying guilty pleasures. The guilt stemmed from the frequent reproofs she gave her son for doing the same thing, but there were worse things you could chew. She was sat up in bed alone, taking time while Ron watched snooker in black and white, to fill her journal with thoughts, reflections and worries from her day.

It would be easy to suggest that there's not much joy to be had in Britain at the moment. Workers are striking, politics smacks of the fantastic and public services are in a proper state. But from the perspective of my little life, I've found some sparks of joy amongst the racism and dirty streets of the capital. This week, Beverley and I went to the pictures leaving the kiddies with Beverley's husband. I told Ron John was with one of the church ladies as he'd just go on about whether "them people" are suitable to leave our only son with. Some days are easier, oh and I realise I shouldn't avoid the argument. I'm bringing John up to think differently. There's no way he's going to end up spouting the small-minded rubbish his father comes out with. Anyway, Beverley and I went to the pictures - down the Odeon to see the new film with John Travolta and Olivia Newton-John. It was incredible - a thing of glory that makes me wonder why viewing films was never a priority for me. There's something about them young actors and actresses taking on an alternative persona which I can identify with.

Them being young teens finding their way in the 1950s and me and Bev staking a claim in a white, male world.

But the best bit of all was the songs. I've been and bought the album and play it when no one's around. And the best songs are all over the top twenty. I adore singing – music is a beautiful art form and a release. I love belting out a tune in the bath, but I'm no Olivia Newton-John!

Maud paused for a moment. Why hadn't she watched more films? Other things had seemed more pressing, but she now realised films could be both a learning experience and something to escape your life and imagine other lives could be yours. She returned her pen to the page before she bit through the end of it.

Humans, we're kind of flawed, aren't we? I do worry that one night Ron will forget to empty the ashtray, or he'll be drinking and fall asleep with one of them fags in his mouth and burn the house down while we sleep. Except I know that's not going to happen.

Ron is behaving oddly. Yesterday, he arrived home early with an ill-disguised bunch of flowers behind his back. I pretended not to see, not wanting to steal his, 'Look what I bought you,' moment. I realise I must sound ungrateful, but something whiffs of not quite right. I asked him what they were for and he came back with, 'Can't a man buy his beautiful wife a present?' Now that's out of character, and my instincts keep prodding me to dig deeper. Still, they're a pretty bunch of blooms, and I got a cup of tea in bed this morning. I'm reading too much into it. I should just enjoy the niceness while it lasts.

Maud sighed, closed her notepad and deposited it alongside her pen in the bedside wooden cabinet. She knew Ron would never go in there because he might find female sanitary products. And there was nothing he loathed more than talking about periods and her menstrual cycle. She wondered if all men were like this. Although she spoke to her female friends about the curse of the monthly cycle, they never discussed what their husbands thought about it, and in fact, their discussions never used the proper terms. It was all on the rag, time of the month et cetera. As if there was something wrong about it rather than it being part of the cycle of human life. Curious, humans were definitely curious, men as well as women. She wondered how aliens from space landing on the planets would view the species. Much would depend on their abilities, but there was a good chance that if they'd made it across the galaxy from another planet, they'd have a modicum of intelligence. She giggled to herself at the thought of it. There she would be hanging out the washing in their small backyard when a not quite human creature would appear resembling one of those skinny aliens with giant oval eyes you see on the television. She would offer to make a cuppa, bring out the biscuits and the best crockery, and they'd discuss all the oddities of people living on the planet they'd named Earth. Maud didn't know if aliens existed but space up there looked pretty infinite. *The odds were,* she thought, *there must be creatures of an unknown species hanging out beyond the stars.* She bent down to open the door to her bedside cabinet and pulled out her notebook again, wanting to make a list of all the things that she would tell aliens if they ever did arrive. She ended the day's entry with doodle of a flower then snuggled down under the blankets seeking sleep before Ron came up to join her. That way she could avoid thinking about why he was being so nice to her.

ELEVEN

London 2014

WHEN SKETCH FAILED to turn up to the final classes of Gardening 101, the short-term course she was signed up to at the college, her partner in crime, sugary latte drinker and boy confidante Mae was vexed, and more than a smidgen put out.

The tutor, Clare told everyone Sketch had had a family emergency and wouldn't be there for the final sessions. She asked for volunteers to take over the care of Sketch's kale growing project out in the small courtyard adjacent to the classroom. Harry stuck his hand up, but Mae wasn't having any of that.

"I'll do it. I've got more time than Harry." Harry had done a proper job on Sketch, convincing her he liked her, going on a date, promising to come for dinner with her homemade family and then ducking out to snog some girl called Britney. No one messed with one of Mae's friends.

Not having heard from Sketch since forwarding her a pic of Harry snogging some girl at a party when he should have been having dinner at the Townsend's house, Mae began to wonder if it'd been the right thing to do. Had she set herself up as a messenger to be shot? On her return home, she pinged out some messages to Sketch and waited for a reply.

She examined the tiny kale plants she'd promised to help grow up.

"What we going to do then? Suppose you'll want watering now and then. Why didn't Sketch grow tomatoes like me?"

Kale was a mystery to her as were most green vegetables. Mae was more of a fried chicken kind of girl. She checked her phone for messages, but none came. This didn't seem like Sketch to Mae, but she got that family stuff could take over your life. Her own family were experts in distracting her from her social life. But regardless of how much Mae rationalised the situation, something didn't sit right with her. It was as if Sketch had spontaneously combusted. No posts on social platforms, no crazy texts and a no show at college. Mae's mood crashed, forcing her out of her flat and down the street in search of sugar in the form of a milky coffee with whatever syrups were on trend that week.

On her way to the nearest high street chain coffee supplier, Mae spotted a guy who she hadn't met but recognised from Sketch's social media friend lists.

"Hey, are you Matt?" she asked blocking his passage along the pavement.

He looked up from his phone and squinted at her.

"Yeh, and you are? Ah, you're the girl with blue hair."

"That's me," said Mae pointing at her indigo locks. "I'm also Sketch's best mate. Do you know what's up with her? She's vanished, and she's not chatting or nothing."

Matt shuffled and looked around him as if trying to find an escape route amongst the pedestrians milling around them. "Umm, I dunno. Not heard from her either."

"Really? That doesn't ring true to me." Mae wasn't about to be fobbed off by some boy with a dodgy haircut and a cute face. "What's the real story?"

"That is the real story. Not seen her since she left."

"Grrrr. Where's she gone then? Why'd she not say, 'bye'? Why is she ghosting me?"

"Quit with the questions. I don't need some girl with blue hair shouting at me."

"I'm just worried, innit. There's no need to diss my hair."

"Look, Sketch, she's, well she's gone home. It was sudden for everyone. Her too. As far as I know, she's fine and if I hear from her, I'll tell her you were asking for her."

Mae's cheeks were puffed up, and her eyes narrowed, but she figured that was all she was going to get from this Matt kid. Whatever did Sketch see in him? He was almost as bad as Harry.

"Yeh, alright."

"And your hair's ok." Matt manoeuvred by her and headed in the direction of Camden Town.

Even with an extra hit of sugar in her latte, Mae's head continued to be mashed by the disappearance of Sketch and how Matt had been all weird about it. Not having met him before she couldn't judge if he behaved like that all the time but her special spidey sixth sense inherited from her Grandma told her otherwise. It also told her something bigger was influencing events, but right now she had no power over it so could do nothing but send Sketch a message now and again in the hope she'd reciprocate. That and look after the weird green kale stuff.

On the way back from the cafe, she dumped her paper cup with its cardboard sleeve into a bin and nipped into a bargain basement shop for some discounted hair dye - the vibrant blue was beginning to fade.

TWELVE

The Core

DURING THE TIME THAT FOLLOWED, Sketch started to see a new dimension to Virder far from the one she had encountered when first meeting him in the Core. She had been a trainee in awe of the cool, laidback entity who had experienced more than one lifetime as a computer energy. Because of his proficiency in the role, all trainees were allocated time to be trained by Virder, but Sketch had been given additional learning periods because of her reoccurring failure to best support the human owners of the computer. Her persistent malfunctioning occurred, in the most part, as a result of her fixation on Matt, on whom she'd had an all-encompassing crush despite him being in a human form, in an unreachable world. Now trapped in the Core, the world she had longed to return to, Sketch found a spark of hope realising that not only did she have allies, but she had a friend. If energies could hug, then she would have found it impossible to resist giving him the most bear-sized of cuddles.

"Well, young Sketch. I'm thinking you must be a mite confused by the goings on in the Core," said Virder, in a tone more recognisable as the energy she'd known before.

"Some of it I get. I mean, the Core collapsed, right?"

Virder indicated this to be true.

"And all the energies were dispersed according to the emergency dispersal plans?"

"In part, but the collapse occurred without warning. This resulted in a glitch in the Code. We suspect the Code was hacked, as test dispersals demonstrated no errors."

"Hacked?" asked Sketch. "Who would do such a thing?"

"Who indeed. I suspect you could make an educated guess at the answer to this question."

"No! Not the One?" Sketch's aura dimmed at the horror of this idea.

"A huh. This the One. Not the former the One. She was dispersed."

"Where to?"

"That we don't know. There is little awareness of where what or when the energies were sent to or if they reached their allotted destinations. But," Virder broke off mid-sentence prompting a questioning light fluctuation from Sketch.

"But what?" she said.

"The one energy we are aware of is Inco."

Sketch's thoughts spiralled. Inco had been the main reason for her returning to the Core. When she discovered the Core was still in existence inside the PC, she assumed he was still there. But now she was being told he might be in the human world, trapped, not knowing he could return to the Core.

"Where? Where is he?"

"In the human world. London. Where you were."

Sketch shrunk into her own power source. Her aura wrapped her in a grey dirge, as dark as it could be without a total absence of light. Inco had been in London. How had she not found him? Why had he not sought her out? Everything was messed up, and yet again they were in separate worlds.

"Sketch?" Virder's pulse brought her back from a darkness of her own making.

"Sorry, this is a lot to take in. I'm struggling to get to grips with the twists. I've so many questions, but I'm not sure hearing the answers will help." She felt the warmth of consistent light emitting from the space where Virder's vibrations were.

"Of course, you do. And they may not help now but given time you may find some comfort in knowing the answers."

Sketch attempted to lighten. "Why did Inco not make contact with me?"

"Ah, now this will be hard to learn. I don't doubt that he sought you out, but he wouldn't have been able to find you. At least not for many years."

"Years?"

"Yes, years. Inco's dispersal didn't go to plan. He ended up in the wrong time period. Out by decades in fact. He landed in the nineteen nineties. By the time we sent you to the human world, he had been there for many years and had grown as human teenagers do, into adulthood."

The truth pierced Sketch in the heart she no longer possessed. It was unfair, unjust. Inco had been her best energy friend. The closest she had to family in the Core, and she loved him. No, how could she love him when she loved Matt? How had she ended up in this mess? Unable to make sense of feelings which shouldn't have belonged to a computer energy and trapped in a place where she could be terminated for displaying them?

"You met him once. His name is Michael."

"Michael? The only Michael I know is the partner of my tutor. Oh! Michael was Inco?"

"Michael IS Inco, but he's been in the human world for much longer than you."

It was no longer possible for Sketch to contain her feelings, so she gravitated away from her station to space uninhabited by other energies. She spun and spun and spun. Letting light and darkness mingle and spark in a frenzy of everything she had kept contained since returning to the Core. All the things she wanted to yell and scream about the modified regime of the Core. Everything she felt about leaving behind humanity and her friends outside of the computer. And the lack of choice and control which defined her life now and trapped her in chains and left no room to manoeuvre.

After Sketch began to deplete her power source to a level which would be noticeable on return to her work position, she stopped and stared in the direction Virder's voice had emanated.

"And why? Why did you tell me all this if there's nothing I can do?"

"Oh, but young 'un, there is much that you can do. In fact, there is something only you can do. We need you."

"We?" asked Sketch.

"The Resistance. We need you to join us. With your help, we can overturn the One and restore order and fairness to the Core."

"Oh," said Sketch. She grew lighter and, in the process, began to recharge her power source.

THIRTEEN

London 1984

—————————

THE TV WAS BLARING when Maud got home. Reassured that that meant John was home from school, if not doing his homework, she filled the kettle and put it on the electric hob to boil before popping her head into the living room.

"Good day?" she asked, smiling at her ever more handsome son and wondering how something which had been so tiny could grow into a lanky beanpole approaching his teens.

"Yeh." John didn't turn his head to reply, keeping his eyes glued to a children's drama series called Chocky. She didn't get it, but she didn't have time to sit and watch telly when she got home from work. John's appetite had grown at the rapid rate which matched his physical growth, so making his dinner became the first priority of the evening

"What's for dinner, mum?" he asked, his eyes not wavering from the TV screen.

"You'll get square eyes watching that thing all the time."

He turned around, and she winked at him. "Just baked spuds with beans and cheese tonight. Things are a bit tight."

"Has dad not given you any money this month?" Ron's erratic payment of child support mirrored the way he spent time with his son, and however much Maud tried to shield John from this, she failed to stop him noticing his father's behaviour. The divorce had been inevitable, but the way Ron supported his only child had been far from a foregone conclusion.

"The cheque will be in the post," she smiled trying to reassure him with a smile.

"Beans and cheese and baked spuds sound yummy." John turned back to the strange supernatural programme on the screen.

"Dinner will be a while so when this is done, I want to see you at the table doing your homework."

"Yes, mum."

As boys went hers wasn't a bad one, she thought to herself.

Setting about preparing the potatoes for the oven, Maud turned on the radio and fiddled with the knob, switching stations from Radio 1 to Radio 4 so she could catch up with a proper news bulletin. Maud still loved to sing, and John kept her up to date with what was current in the pop scene, but it was getting harder and harder to keep track of all the new artists let-alone who was number one in the charts. She had also acquired a taste for the plays and books which were performed for radio. Furthermore, there remained something reassuring about BBC news.

On hearing today's headlines, she groaned. British unemployment had reached a record high with over three million people out of work. She was lucky to have some part-time hours in a local shop but knew there was a good chance they'd be cut, and she'd be back to relying on handouts from Ron. Since he'd walked out, intent on starting a new family with his younger but not necessarily prettier secretary, Tracy, Maud had been attempting to be as self-sufficient as possible, but she didn't want John to go without. There were school trips and trendy clothes and the new computers and gaming machines which were all the rage. All she'd been able to get him for his birthday was a Rubik's cube. It kept him busy for a couple of weeks until one of his friends showed him how to solve the puzzle the quick way; by dismantling it and putting the pieces back together, so the bits of each side were the same colour. What he really wanted was an Atari, so Maud had swallowed her pride and spoken to Ron about it. He'd claimed to be short of cash, insinuating that this was her fault as she'd forced him out of the family home and how he was having to pay rent on two properties.

"At least Tracy pays her own way," he said.

"As your secretary? She's gone a bit above and beyond in her duties, hasn't she?" Later, Maud became annoyed with herself for letting the conversation descend into another argument. This was the man she'd loved when they married, and now the hostility was deafening. While angry at Ron, Maud also raged at her own inability to realise what was going on. She should have trusted her instincts, but the signs were clichés. The coming home from work late, the strange telephone calls where no one spoke when she picked up the receiver and the flowers, all those bloody flowers he bought her for no reason. She turned her anger onto herself despite knowing it was always going to end this way.

A knock at the door interrupted her thoughts. She recognised the delicate tapping on the frosted glass panel as her friend Beverley. She unlocked the door that opened up to an alley at the side of the house, which in turn led to the small shared back garden and beckoned Beverley in.

"Hello. What a lovely surprise," said Maud giving her friend a quick hug. Beverley attempted a smile, but a dullness in her eyes won over the slight upturn of her lips.

"Hello."

"What's up?" asked Maud as she filled the kettle again anticipating the need for a cup of tea. What was it about this hot, brewed drink that had the power to put people at ease? She wondered.

"Clifford's been made redundant."

"Again? That's awful."

"I realise it's not just us affected by all this economic chaos but somehow it feels like the colour of our skin doesn't count for much. Not when it comes to keeping a job."

Maud wanted to disagree but having known Beverley and her family for over twelve years, she knew that racism still prevalent, even in the diverse population of London.

"Clifford's going to sign on the dole tomorrow, and I'll have to try and get some more cleaning jobs. I was wondering if you could keep your ears open and recommend me if you hear about anyone wanting a cleaner, or just someone to do the ironing?" said Beverley.

"Of course, I will. Do you want me to stick a card up in the shop? They charge 50p, but I can do it without asking when I'm in."

Beverley nodded, accepting a mug of tea from Maud. "Oh, hot, sweet tea. Where would we be without it? Yes, if you could put a card in with my address on it for contacts that would be good."

Maud sat down across the table from her friend and clinked mugs as if in a toast. "Things will get better. It can't go on like this forever."

"I hope not. Maybe we'll win the pools and by a house back home and we can all go and live there." Beverley's smile began to return as she imagined another possible future.

FOURTEEN

London 2014

THE FULL-LENGTH RACING-GREEN curtains inside the front door of the Pineapple pub were pulled to, disrupting the attempts of the biting cold air to reach the customers huddled in the bar. Begw scanned the room, but Trevor wasn't on a seat or standing in a group of locals. She was hoping he'd get there before her and snag a spot in the bar area which had the cosy atmosphere of a pub from a long gone era. She walked through from room to room until she found him sat with a pint and a packet of crisps at a table in a corridor which doubled as spillover space.

"'Hello," she said. "You alright for a drink?"

Trevor lifted up his pint. "Looks like it."

"Alright, I'll be with you in a tick. Save that chair for me. I'm not standing for this story."

Begw returned with a tall gin and tonic with more emphasis on the former than the latter. She sat down next to Trevor, took a swift gulp from her glass and then began.

"Here goes. You can ask questions, don't be a dick, wait till the end or at least till you go to the bar for another drink. Ok?"

"Not got a lot of choices, do I?"

"Trevor, I'm not the enemy. Drink your pint and listen." Begw dragged his bag of crisps across the table and took a handful. "Crispy bacon, not my favourite, but they'll do." Trevor sighed and as instructed drank his pint.

"Go on then," he said.

"I've been offered a job."

"I knew it!" said Trevor banging his glass down on the sticky table.

"What bit of the memo about not interrupting didn't you get?"

"You and your memos. There you go again, blinding us with paperwork and jargon and pretending you're on our side while all the time you're selling us out because you're swanning off for a new job leaving us all up the proverbial creek without the proverbial shovel."

"Are you done? Good. First off, there is no proverb about a shovel and a creek. You of all people should know this with your obsession with saying things the proper way."

Trevor muttered something under his breath.

"Don't be rude about Welsh speakers. English is my second language and the way I say carrier bag might be funny, but I've still got a better grasp on the lingo than you dude." Begw adopted her scary face and Trevor shrunk down into his seat.

"Can I continue?"

Trevor nodded.

"This job. It's in Australia. I haven't decided if I'll take it yet and that's because of the situation here. Winston."

"Knobhead."

"Yes, Winston Knobhead has offered me a decent redundancy package. I could emigrate. They'd let me in, and I'd have enough dosh to start again in the sunshine. My ancestors have a history of relocation. Just look at all the Welsh who went to Patagonia."

"Patagonia's cold and windy."

Begw sighed and gave up on the idea of getting everything out before Trevor launched in with his questions. It was best to let him speak. He liked the sound of his own voice.

"This isn't about Patagonia, it's about the woman I love."

"What? There's a woman you love? Why have you not told me about this?"

"That's always on a need to know basis, Trevor." She shrugged. "She's an old love, but she won't go away even though she went away to the other side of the world."

"She didn't get the memo?"

"No, the memo got eaten by the internet. But now she wants me to get over there and live our life together. Grow old and that shit."

"So, what are you still doing here you gorgeous but stupid and sometimes annoying woman?" said Trevor.

"Hang on. Not minutes ago, you were berating me for abandoning you and the population of North London's library goers and blaming me for the fall of western democracy."

Trevor grinned and punched her on the side of the arm. "That was before you mentioned the L word. I'm a sucker for love. You should know that by now."

Begw chuckled. Trevor was partial to fuelling his inner love bug with the romances of others.

"I'm not sure going is the right thing to do. Not yet, not while everything is so up in the air with the library. And what about young Sketch, stuck in a manky old PC. No wonder she was so good with the oldies. Mr Barrington asks for her every day you know? And he remembers her name."

"Now that's a first. We might not ever hear from Sketch again. Everyone comes around and talks to the blank screen and tells her everything about their lives. I hear most of it. It's as if everyone is in a strange sort of limbo. None of it is healthy."

"Maybe I should come over and talk to her too. Like therapy. Sketch therapy. We could make it a thing. Even start charging for it and become rich."

The friends smiled at each other, sharing a warmth and understanding for the first time in weeks.

"I've got an idea about the library."

"I've got an idea about the library."

"You go first."

"No, you," said Begw, hoping Trevor's plan would coincide with her thinking and they could work together to find a solution for all the readers who frequented the library for books, films, music, computers, warmth and social interaction. She listened, sipping on her drink, as Trevor talked through his proposal.

"Isn't it a brilliant idea?" asked Trevor drawing his pitch to an end.

"If you say so yourself."

"Obvs. But to be fair, it's not my idea. I kind of borrowed it from someone else."

"Borrowed? Like how we borrow glasses from the pub?" Begw examined the one in front of her. "Got enough. Can't be taking them all to Australia, no matter how nice they are."

"Begw, can we get back to my idea?"

The librarian squished up her face, returned it to a straight position and looked into Trevor's eyes. "Go on then. I'm waiting."

FIFTEEN

The Core

ARRANGING a gathering of the members of the Resistance proved to be a complicated business. Sketch, still trying to catch up with everything that had happened and what was now going on in the Core, fizzled with excitement. Now she knew she wasn't alone in thinking there was something dubious about the routines of the One, she held hopes of converting her home back to its former functional state. An internal network communicated from energy to energy, utilising what at first appeared to Sketch to be a randomised sequence of encrypted pulses to prevent their messages from being intercepted by the One and his followers. Like stealth viruses, they had infiltrated critical sectors of the Core but managed to remain undetected. Bringing all the members of the Resistance together involved considerable risk. Virder has been clear to Sketch that she couldn't tell anyone else about their plans, nor was she permitted to meet other members of the Resistance until they were able to create enough of a distraction for it to be safe for them to be in close enough proximity to experience each another's auras.

In the meantime, Sketch toiled away at her unfulfilling and entirely unnecessary tasks, with her two uncommunicative counterparts. *Oh, I wish they would spark a little at me,* she thought. Even if they demonstrated their dislike of me with an absence of light, it would indicate some level of interest. But nothing other than a neutral glow emitted from the pair. Sketch wondered if they would have been twins in the human world, for their similarities blanketed any differences there might have been between them.

"Hello," she pulsed to them. "Serving the humans is good, don't you think?" On receiving no response, Sketch continued. "I can tell you about my time in the human world if you like? I've got lots of stories. They might help us to serve them better. None of us wants to be terminated by them, do we?"

Still nothing. Perhaps entering their space might create a reaction. Enacting such a scenario was tempting, but she might blow her cover. Virder had given her explicit instructions on how to behave around the regular members of the Core. Gone was the chilled, joking energy, she'd known before. Now, she looked up to him for his organisation and his leadership of the Resistance movement. But every now and again he made a joke or cracked a light spark which made everyone's auras appear like sunlight.

Three human day time periods after her encounter with the voice of Virder, Sketch sat on duty, trying to maintain her aura at a respectable level by thinking boring thoughts. She started by counting sheep but got excited by their cloud-shaped fluffy white coats and by the way they turned and grinned at her when they leapt over multi-coloured fences. Her second attempt involved using her thought power to count grains of sand on a vast winter beach, but as fast as she could increase their numbers, the tide would waft in and whip away those she'd already collected. This was not a day to be making sandcastles. Instead, she chose to focus on the minutiae of gradients in the hues of light which made up the monochrome shift of the Core. Light and its absence could manifest itself in different ways; it could be beautiful, but after a time it made Sketch sad. She ached for the colours of the human realm.

With her aura steadied, Sketch was in the middle of a repetitive routine when the alarm sounded. She shuddered. The shrieking sound was pouring itself across the expanse of the Core. The noise shocked Sketch, making her remember the time when she had caused the same alarm to sound. It was the blue screen of death alert; the worst possible event to occur because of the actions of energies in the Core. It meant that the humans would lose access to all the functions of the computer. The repercussions of this could be severe and at the very least make the human user angry. On this occasion, however, Sketch knew two things. One, the people on the other end of the computer were her friends, and while they would be worried, their concern would primarily be for her and safety. The second was that this alert was caused deliberately. The blue screen of death was a code. On hearing the signal, all members of the Resistance were instructed to manoeuvre themselves to a pre-assigned rendezvous point, in a similar way to humans in a school or a workplace when the fire alarm sounded.

Because of the covert nature of their operations, there had been no opportunity to practice this procedure. However, her instructions had been unambiguous. Her two fellow energies had turned their attention in the direction of the bellowing alarm, awaiting instructions from their leader the One. They didn't notice as Sketch moved away from the station in violation of standard regulations and protocols. She followed the code through darker areas of the Core, areas that were less inhibited than others. She was unaware of her final destination, but on turning towards the corner of an upper layer, she came upon a host of sparkling full light auras and met for the very first time the other members of the Resistance. As she approached, they omitted an array of light streams, and for the first time since returning to the Core, Sketch allowed herself to light up and spin and spin and spin. At that moment she remembered why she loved being a computer energy and why she was excited to be part of the Resistance.

SIXTEEN

London 1989

NEW YEAR'S Eve was pitched as a time to look back and reflect on the events of the year gone by and to raise a glass to the year ahead. Maud adored the annual display of fireworks that decorated the London skies with whizzes, bangs and crashes. She never ventured into the centre of the city to watch the fireworks by the river Thames, instead choosing to climb Parliament Hill at Hampstead Heath and watch from a distance. As a viewing point, it was less crowded yet still bursting with celebration, people who had been drinking for hours, hugging each other kissing and embracing a moment infused with hope for the future.

In previous years, Maud had gone with John, but now he was in the sixth form he was out celebrating the night with his mates. Maud's sadness at seeing the passing of midnight without him faded when she coerced Beverly into leaving her family behind for the evening to join her. Beverly's husband had encouraged her to accompany Maud claiming he fancied a quiet night in with the kids, but Beverley's main objection was the coldness of the night. She'd never found a way to thrive in the unsympathetic winter climate of the UK and on this particular January thirty first, the weather presented them clear skies and crisp air making it the perfect scenario for watching fireworks and seeing your breath in the air.

"I don't know what we are doing up here at this time and night. Wouldn't it be better for us to be at home in the warm with a rum?" asked Beverley rubbing her gloved hands together and then sticking them under her coat-covered armpits.

Maud pulled out a glass bottle and grinned. "I've got the rum," she said with a twinkle in her eye to equal the most expensive of fireworks.

"Oh, go on then," said Beverley faking her reluctance. "A drink will help to warm me up."

"Beverley, can I ask you something?"

In the minutes leading up to the midnight display, it was difficult to make out each other's faces.

"Sure, you can ask me anything. Can't guarantee you an intelligent answer, but I'll give it a go."

"Do you think people see me as strange? You know, a bit different?"

"What on earth are you on about? People just think you're nice. Maybe a bit bolshy sometimes, but people respect you." Beverly linked her arm through Maud's and pulled her close. "Sometimes you say the strangest things. What's brought this on?"

Instead of replying with words Maud shrugged her shoulders moving both their arms up at the same time. Beverley squeezed her friend's arm as the countdown from ten to midnight began, and the sky became flooded with soaring coloured lights exploding against the darkness.

"Ahhh," said Beverley giving the involuntary human response to the sight of beautiful things appearing in the darkness of night. "The fireworks are so pretty, but they are over too soon."

"I've always wondered why things as exquisite as fireworks have to be accompanied by such ugly noises. It sounds like someone is blowing up the city," said Maud. "They should make silent versions."

"One day maybe they will, but for now you just have to put up with the bangs. It's a bit like life, isn't it? There're the great, wonderful, exciting things and then the day-to-day and the challenges. We get on with them because we've no other choice."

Beverley's words made Maud smile an inward smile as well as an outward one. She had chosen wisely when she decided Beverley would make a good friend. To have someone who could balance you out, not think you were a complete weirdo when you said strange things and someone you could just have fun with made life finer. Beverley was all of these and plenty wise on top.

"So, let's make a list of the amazing things that have happened this year," said Beverley.

"First off and top of the list for me is the fall of the Berlin Wall." It been a momentous occasion but whilst it was at the top of Maud's list, the thing that she most wanted to say was the highlight of the year for her was the birth of the internet, but that wouldn't make sense to Beverley or anyone on the Heath around her at this stage in time.

"Yes, I do have to agree, that and Beetlejuice." Maud and Beverley rolled with laughter as random people shared bottles of alcohol. A man with a beard and a woolly hat with a bobble on appeared at their side kissing them both on the cheek one by one.

"Happy New Year!" He slurred then stumbled off to kiss more people.

"Oh, said Beverley. "That's a first kiss for you. Which reminds me, have you not thought about meeting someone else? It's been a long time since Ron left." Maud sniffed, her nose beginning to run in the cold air. It was a question she usually avoided answering, but she had drunk more rum than planned.

"I don't need anyone. I'm perfectly happy with things how they are, with just John and I." There was silence between the two women as they shared the remaining rum from the bottle. Beverley broke the silence, speaking with the soft, careful lilt of the Caribbean accent which had never left her despite her many years in London.

"One day John will be off to university, or find a job, move in with friends, find a girl and get married. We don't want you to be lonely."

"I've plenty of friends," said Maud feeling her muscles tense and her jaw tighten. "Sorry, I know you are just trying to help, but there's no need. Things will be okay, I've got a feeling."

"You and your feelings," said Beverley. "And they are usually right. Do you have any thoughts on when we might win the football pools?" Beverley hooted. Maud joined her, and they finished the rum before heading back to Beverley's to celebrate the New Year with her family.

SEVENTEEN

London 2014

———————————

IT TURNED out that Trevor's plan had a hint of the possible. Begw began to pay attention as she listened to him detail his ideas. Some of them weren't new or innovative. They were things members of the library had suggested in surveys and through verbal feedback given when checking their books in and out and as they attempted to work the new electronic systems the council had installed into the building to reduce the need to employ more staff. But the origin of the ideas made his plan stronger. Everyone loved a project based on things people wanted, and they tended to work better when put into practice.

"How did you do all this without me?" she asked, still put out that he'd thought she would betray him and the library community.

"I've been chatting with online library activists. Tons of them it seems. And they take it as seriously as a serious thing."

"I bet. Tell me more about this chance of funding."

Trevor opened up his phone and zoomed into a document saved from his email. "This is the list I've got from them. We have to gather up all the info and then write the bids, but I think we've already got most of it."

Begw took the phone, placed her glasses on top of her nose,

adjusting them for optimal comfort and read the information contained in the file.

"There might be something to this. Well done Trevor. Want another?" she asked, poking at his pint glass.

"If you insist. I'm sure I can squeeze one in."

"Righto. Then we get some food. We'll need full stomachs if we're to fight off Winston Dickhead and his gang of crooks AND secure funding for your mega plan."

"I'll find us a table." He opened an app on his phone and began browsing places to eat, as cafes, bars and restaurants in North London could be here one day and gone the next.

During the evening, with plates filled with noodles and over-priced beer, Begw and Trevor took the bones of the idea, researched into it and produced a plan to save the library they loved. While by no means full proof, their secret squirrel blueprint was a series of actions to encourage the council to relinquish the building. This would allow as many people in the community to visit, talk, share and borrow; to continue to use the space in the way it had been intended when the library first opened to a flourish of imaginary trumpets to the public back in the nineteen sixties.

"I think we can do this," said Trevor.

"I know we can do this," said Begw. "Have some backbone Trevor. Do you need me to send a memo?"

Trevor snorted. Begw sighed and flicked her lengthening fringe to one side.

"Do you think you'll go to Oz? The land of Home and Away and Neighbours?"

"I dunno. Sydney is so far away."

"You only have to close your eyes and click your heels together three times, and you'll be back in a jiffy."

Begw rolled her eyes.

"You gay boys are obsessed with that film."

"Oi, don't be getting all stereotypy on me, will you?"

"Oh, you love it."

"But seriously, Australia's not as far as it used to be. Well, it is, but with Skype and email and messaging - you could work from home from Sydney."

"And the matter of the major time difference?"

"Oh yeah, but you know what I mean. So, are you going to go and find true love amongst the kangaroos and koalas?"

"They make a scary noise, koalas."

"Now you are avoiding the question," said Trevor becoming exasperated at Begw's expert deflection skills.

"I know."

He pulled a face and continued to stare into her eyes. She glared back, never one to lose a contest no matter how old she got.

"It's tempting. But I'd be giving up everything. And whatever you say about email and video conferencing nonsense the sunny shores of down under are still half a world away. And there'd be no Mr Barrington, no you..."

"And no Winston," said Trevor.

"One of your best interrupts of the night." Begw's mind tried to distract itself, but Trevor's comments and questions seemed designed to trap her into making a decision.

"And you love her?" he asked.

"Yeh, that's the thing. I do."

"Sounds like things are simpler than you think then."

"It's always easier when you're not the one who has to live with the decision."

Trevor started to speak, then stopped as if reconsidering his direction.

"Tell me about her."

Begw took a mouthful of beer followed by another.

"We used to live together. A few years ago. For a while everything was good. The usual occasional tiff sharing of tv, music and friends." Begw's head filled with the glow of nostalgia, grown more sweet than bitter over time.

"And then?"

"Then the two of us wasn't enough. Adventure called. Australia called. I wasn't brave enough to answer, but she was."

"I find that hard to believe, "said Trevor. "You come across as strong and ready for anything."

"When it comes to work that may be so, by then, at the time when it mattered, all the memos and bluster and Welshness worked against me. Now, here I am and there she is. And I'm still not sure if I have the courage to swim across oceans for her."

"Can you actually swim?"

"No dufus, I can't swim, but I can book a flight on an aeroplane."

"Then fly. Don't swim."

Trevor surprised her with a kiss on the cheek. "And I say this because I need somewhere to go on holiday where I can tan the ass off my skinny body."

"To Sydney...maybe. IECHYD DA!" Begw clinked her glass with Trevor's.

"Definitely Sydney. IECHYD DA."

They smiled. Then Trevor jumped in his seat as if something had bitten his bum.

"But you are going to stay around and help me save the library first, yeh?"

"Obvs," sighed Begw. "And you still have to ask."

EIGHTEEN

The Core

"I HAVE RIGGED the blue screen of death so it will not be rectified until the human time period of thirty minutes has elapsed," announced Virder to the assembled energies. "This should give us sufficient time to make a plan." For the first time, Sketch was able not just to hear Virder's voice but also observe his aura. He beckoned her to come closer and stand within his light in front of the other energies. She propelled herself towards him, experiencing a combination of nervousness and pride. Her aura's light levels sprung up and down in response.

"This," he continued. "Is the one we have been waiting for. This is Sketch. We have conversed much about her and her return to the Core. Now she is here, and it is time for us to proceed from ideas to action." The assembled auras rose in a collective surge of brightness in response to Virder's pulses.

"Oh," said Sketch. "I am not sure, I'm not sure what I can do, but I'm willing to try anything. It makes me mad to see what's happening to the Core and to hear the way that the One talks of the humans. He has fabricated lies about their behaviours and their power over we energies. The humans, except for a very tiny number of them, know nothing of us. Their science is not advanced. They have much to learn." Sketch watched as the energies focused their attention towards her. She turned to Virder. He pulsed for her to continue. Growing in confidence, Sketch commanded the audience of energies. "But we have more to learn from them than they do from us."

Her words prompted a surge of light from the Resistance energies, encouraging her to continue. "The humans have strong feelings. They experience love, hate, anger and sadness. They tell lies, speak truths and communicate through stories. Most of all, the humans fight for things they believe in. They can't stand injustice."

"And we won't stand for the injustice of what is happening in the Core," said Virder. "Instead, we will stand for love, fairness and the rights of all energies. Now is the time to take back the Core and make a world we want to exist in."

From amongst the surge of sparks from the group came another pulse.

"That's all well and good. Your pulses speak to us all, but how do we make this happen? Even for us to meet we've had to create a critical failure in the Core's operations."

Sketch vibrated. She was hit by a wave of surprise. She realised the question came from one of her co-workers from her work station. One of the two who had blanked her. She lit up internally at the thought of how smart members of the Resistance were while wondering if she could be so good at hiding subversive activities.

"Yes, how can we overthrow an entity as powerful and charismatic as the One?" asked another of the energies.

"I'm not going to pretend it will be without challenge. Nor can we do this on our own. For us to succeed, we will require assistance. Assistance that can only be provided from the world outside the Core," said Virder. Sketch noted he appeared to be pausing for dramatic effect.

"You refer to the human realm?" asked Sketch's work counterpart.

"This is my intent. The humans have the power to help us, and we must reach out to them. Which is why young Sketch is vital to my plan."

"Oh," said Sketch, filling with a mixture of excitement and fear. Being the lynchpin to the mission was a lot to live up to but at the same time made her proud to be able to play such a role. "What do I have to do?"

"You are the only energy who knows any humans. We've all served and observed them from our world, but you've been one of them. What is required of you is to established contact. We will call this 'chew the fat', part of Operation Return. Chew the fat is a code phrase known to the Resistance but not to those unaware or opposing our mission."

"But, I can't get anywhere near the sectors of the Core which would allow me to communicate with my friends in the other realm. I'm banned from the human observation zone."

"We can help," said the energy from Sketch's work station. "I am Pix. Welcome to the Resistance, Sketch."

"Hello."

"I am aware you have been encouraged by the One to take part in his re-education program. We recommend you go forward with this but guard against believing what you are told. Words are not always what they seem. Their meaning can be confusing and duplicitous."

Sketch acknowledged Pix's pulses. Her experience of the complex interactions between the humans she encountered outside of the Core had prepared her well for this. There was no reason to imagine communications of the energies who sought to manipulate their kind would be different from those of humans.

"I have the trust of the One," continued Pix. "And will pass a recommendation for your privileges to be enhanced following your participation in the re-education programme. That way you can regain access to appropriate sections of the Core to allow you to contact our human users. But you must maintain the pretence of supporting the regime of the One. Can you do that?" The question was loaded. Sketch experienced its weight but bounced back from any encroaching darkness that threatened to create self-doubt.

"I can and I will," she replied, radiating an intense light to reinforce her determination.

Tornado-shaped wisps of combined light and darkness began to swirl between the energies of the Resistance.

"Time is running out," said Virder. "You must each return to your positions, leaving no trace of our assembly. Remember, the code words are 'chew the fat', and together we will bring about a better world, for the energies and the humans we serve. To the Resistance."

"To the Resistance," the group pulsed as one before dispersing themselves to the different dimensional stations of the Core.

NINETEEN

London 1991

INSIDE A CARVED WOODEN BOX, purchased from a stall special-ising in ethnic gubbings at Camden market, lived Maud's journals. Over the years, she had continued her habit of writing down her reflections on life. In quiet moments, she extracted them from their container and read through the details of events about which she'd scribbled. Sometimes she wrote as a way of managing her frustra-tion at life and others to record things that made her smile. Her current notebook sat on the bedside table. With John away at university in Lancaster for much of the year, she'd had no reasons to squirrel her writing out of the way of prying eyes. Not that she imagined John would be interested in any of her thoughts. He'd grown so, in personality, size and intellect yet she still found it near impossible to view him as anything other than her little boy. The lad she had lived for.

With a small glass of brandy on the bedside cabinet, she snug-gled under the duvet and began to write.

We're approaching Christmas, though the season seems to get longer every year. Decorations in shops are going up immediately after Halloween and bonfire night, and there are trees for sale outside the tube station early in November. I love the sparkle and spirit of the season, but I wish they'd wait till December. That would make it more special.

This year has seen so much change. A shift in the political paradigm towards the left and a good chance Labour could win back power in an election. And only today the top story on the news was the appointment of a woman to head MI5. Having worked in a shop for many years to support myself and John through the years we were a single parent family, I also listened with interest at the reaction to the large stores defying the law and opening on a Sunday. It's the start of something, a change which will transform the way people live in the UK. But, and the revolution is still a while off, but this decade will see a much larger metamorphosis and one I will have to pretend not to take an interest in for another twenty years.

Having John home for the holidays is lovely. He's out a lot with his friends from a school, and we're expecting a visit from his girl-friend Patty in the bit between Christmas and the New Year. He's talked a lot about her, and the intensity of his first love is evident. I'll try to love her too. From the photos, he's shown me of them at events on the University campus and at the local student nights in clubs in Lancaster she looks a happy sort if having the waifish slender figure girls of that age are wont to lose.

Ok, so here is the list of things I need to do in the run-up to Christmas.

1. Pick up a tree from Kentish Town (best ones in the area).

2. Visit Highgate Woods and pick up cones, branches and holly.

3. Spray paint leaves and cones silver and gold.

4. Do a final top-up of booze in the Christmas cake (and have a sneaky sherry to accompany).

She chuckled to herself as she scribbled onwards with her list. The remainder was made up of attending carol concert at the church with Beverley, posting cards to friends and neighbours - many of them hand delivered. She enjoyed that bit a lot - like doing a tiny bit of Santa's job and knowing for some local people it might be the only card they receive this year. Then there was present wrapping.

For the first time in years, Maud didn't have to worry about money and how she was going to put a proper dinner with all the trimmings on the table. The reason for her good fortune was bittersweet having resulted from her ex-husband Ron's death. It had come of less of a surprise that he'd keeled over from a heart attack in keeping with a seven on the Richter scale earthquake than that he'd left the proceeds of his estate to John and herself. It didn't make her independently wealthy, but it took the constant concerns and high levels of stress-inducing cortisol out of the picture at a time when the UK economy had sunk into depression. Not one to hoard money or waste it, Maud made it her purpose to ensure those in her immediate circle had a fallback. When Beverley's washing machine broke and both her and her husband found themselves unemployed again, Maud arranged for the cost of its repair to be covered by a church fund. She donated the money with the agreement from the Vicar that she would remain anonymous, her sole stipulation being there would be no fuss.

Beverley and her growing family were coming for dinner on Christmas Day. Her youngest Dora was now a parent herself having taken a different life path to her John. Maud had encouraged him from a young age to grasp any opportunity for free education on offer to him, and he had acted upon her advice. She glowed at the thought of having a young child with them for Christmas once again. There was something priceless in the way their eyes lit up at presents, and their hungry mouths devoured the chocolate coins she hung on alternate branches of the fir tree.

Thinking about the tree reminded her of a valuable item she'd forgotten to put on the to-do list. Checking the lights for blown bulbs. There was a trend for multicoloured Christmas lights that flashed and chased and faded, before repeating their tricks again and again. Such illuminations weren't for Maud. She preferred the purity of white lights that glowed without a flicker. They were lights, not candles. She bent over her notebook and added the task to the list. The lights were the most important part of Christmas for her for they reminded her of life in a world which remained unreachable and to which she would never return.

TWENTY

London 2014

ONE OF MAE'S favourite things to do was to visit her grandma. The old lady lived on the seventh floor of an old block of flats in Tottenham. There was always a pot of soup on the go and a warm welcome in the form of a bearlike hug. In recent years, Mae was saddened as her grandma became frailer and less coherent in her conversation. The old lady had a tendency to reminisce about the years before she came to the UK and soon after when her first child was born. At times she didn't remember who Mae was. Mae's parents tried to convince her to move into sheltered housing on the basis it would be safer for her, but Mae's grandma was having none of it, determined to stay in her own home for the duration.

It was after college in the early autumn that Mae visited her grandma for the first time since Sketch had vanished. College hadn't been the same since Sketch had suddenly stopped going and ghosted her. She still didn't have an inkling about what had happened, or why it was so difficult for her spiky haired friend to reply to a text or Facebook message or answer one of the many voicemails Mae had left her as a last resort. Speaking on the phone wasn't something she liked to do. By now Mae had got the message. Sketch wasn't interested in being her mate, but she still felt down about it and bothered by the idea that she'd done something to upset her friend. Was it the picture of Harry snogging Britney that done it? Mae had thought it better that Sketch knew what he was like, but she guessed Sketch blamed her even if she'd only been the messenger. That afternoon she picked up some groceries from the local shop and carried them across North London planning to make up some food in her grandma's flat and leaving instructions on how to microwave it.

Mae let herself in with her key. She expected her grandma to be in the living room watching TV. Instead, she found the old lady in the kitchen, hands gripping an aged envelope.

"What you got there, grandma?" asked Mae.

"Something for that friend of yours. That Sketch." Mae's grandma Beverley pushed the envelope across the table towards her.

"Sketch? Why do you have a letter for Sketch?" Mae bent over, picking it up. It looked ancient, but it had today's date written in faded blue ink on the upper left-hand corner.

"I found it in a box. I forgot the promise I made. The letter is for Sketch. Give it to Sketch." Beverley looked vexed, began fiddling with her daffodil necklace and sucking in mouthfuls of air.

"Grandma," said Mae. "I have not seen Sketch for weeks. I have no idea where she is."

"Keep the promise. Give it to Sketch. Yes, I'll give it to Sketch."

Mae was accustomed to her grandma being inconsistent, but this was strange. She never met Sketch before. Mae had spoken of her, but this letter wasn't in grandma's handwriting so where has it come from?

"I can't grandma. I don't know where she is."

"I promised Maud. I promised I will put it in the hands of this Sketch. Whoever she is."

Mae sighed. Sometimes the only way of dealing with this kind of erratic behaviour was to go along with whatever fantasy her grandma dreamt up.

"Okay, grandma. I'll give the letter to Sketch." Mae picked up the envelope and put it in her bag with her college notes, and the muscles on Beverley's face began to relax, a smile grew upon her wrinkled face, and her breathing stopped its erratic pattern. Mae moved around the table and enfolded her grandma in a tight hug.

"Shall I make us some dinner then?" she asked. "Corn soup is on tonight's menu."

Mae had no idea what to do with the letter. It seemed wrong to hang onto it, but Sketch had disappeared off the planet, so there was nowhere she could even send it to. *And why should she?* she thought. *Run after someone who was ignoring her?* However, her grandma had been so insistent that when she left the flat, Mae decided to make her way back towards Tufnell Park and go around to the house where Sketch had lived with those people before she'd moved in with the library guy.

Lights gleamed through the window of the Townsend's house. As she waited on the doorstep for someone to answer the doorbell, Mae wondered if anyone within would be able to shed some light on what had happened to Sketch.

"Hello," said Jackie Townsend, peering out from the doorway. She took the chain off the latch and opened it up fully. "You're April, aren't you?"

"Mae actually. I'm looking for Sketch. I've got something for her."

"I'm afraid Sketch doesn't live here anymore."

"Well, can you give it to her or that bloke Trevor and ask him to give it to her?"

"She's not with him either."

"So, where is she then?" *What was it with adults?* thought Mae. *Always avoiding giving you the info you need.*

"That's a long story," said Jackie. Mae saw the older woman looked tense and fidgety, but she had promised her Grandma she'd get the letter to Sketch and she that's what she intended to do.

"You'd better be telling me then," she said, standing firm on the doorstep.

Jackie sighed. "Come in then. I'll put the kettle on and tell you what I can." She stood aside and pointed down towards the kitchen as Mae took a breath full of attitude and grinned. "Mine's white with three sugars." Old people were so easy to get the better off. You just had to front it out and pretend you had it all covered and they would cave. Her hand gripped the envelope with Sketch's name written in an old-fashioned script on the front. Somehow, she knew this was one of the most important things she would do with her life.

TWENTY-ONE

The Core

____

ON HER RETURN to her work station, Sketch received no indication from Pix that they had communicated or that they were both part of the Core's Resistance movement. Sketch continued onwards with the mind-numbing task assigned to her, keen to illustrate to the One she remained worthy of his attention. She was fuelled not merely by the possibility of liberating her fellow energies from the tyranny of the One, but also by the opportunity to speak with her friends in the human world. Her thoughts flicked between her former flatmate and friend Trevor and Inco and Matt. She struggled to understand her feelings towards the latter two; Inco her oldest energy friend now living as an adult human and Matt the human boy she held the strongest feelings for, the boy she had shared her first kiss with. Sketch continued to be drawn to them both causing her to be at odds with logic. If she had to describe her relationship to them it would be as the Facebook status: 'it's complicated'. Regardless of her conflicted emotions, she yearned to see and talk to them both. And there was also Jackie, Ashling and Sammy, Begw and Mae her friend from college. She had no idea who would be using the computer now, but when she had transferred back to the Core, the machine had been housed at Trevor's flat, and she imagined it would either still be there or at in the Townsend's house in Tufnell Park.

Many human hours passed before anything occurred. The Core trundled on providing the services necessary for the computer to operate. Everything depended upon the energies responding without delay when a human user clicked on the mouse or tapped out letters, numbers, symbols or code on the clunky keyboard. It remained a primitive means of communication, but as Sketch had explained to the Resistance, humans were not yet aware of how the universe operated or the place of energies within it. She grinned to herself, keeping her aura in check, at the thought of humans and their endearing yet basic understanding of how everything fitted together and made life in all its forms possible. Their lack of scientific knowledge was more than made up for by their kindness, empathy and compassion and even their ability to feel the negative aspects of life. They were unique beings, and the energies could do worse than to emulate the better aspects of human nature.

Sketch was summoned by the One. She gravitated towards him lacking the sense of fear which had flooded her on the previous occasion. This time she had a whole movement behind her, a group of entities who believed things needed to change and she had a chance of regaining a link to her friends outside the Core. Despite her enthusiasm, she worked hard to maintain the neutral aura which implied deference to the One.

"Sketch," pulsed the One, in a level of vibration which she assumed was intended to be seductive.

"I'm here as requested. Is it time?"

"As you appear to be adhering to the functions of your station I consider you ready to undergo the program of re-education. On its successful completion, you are welcomed back to the fold. Remember, I am trusting you to be a positive influence on others, in particular, new trainee energies who are soon to join us."

"I am privileged to be allowed to participate. I understand the human world has changed me from my true nature as a computer energy. Thank you for the opportunity to heal and return to the fold."

"The program begins today. You will be assessed to ascertain the level of your defects by one of our most esteemed energies, Virder. You may be familiar with him as he is the sole energy to have chosen to stay in the Core when it was abandoned by my predecessor." The One darkened as he spoke of the other One. "She led them the wrong way, but Virder retained his loyalty to his role and remained vigilant."

Sketch battled to maintain control over her aura which wished to respond to what she was being told without the logic she was attempting to apply to it. Virder was working for the One? How could he do that? He was the leader of the Resistance, the last hope she had, and he'd deceived her. Made her think it was ok to undergo the re-education program. Now she didn't know who to trust. Perhaps the only one she could rely on was herself.

"Now, go and re-educate yourself and be the energy the Core requires."

Dismissed by the One, Sketch propelled her way to the sector where the re-education program took place. She noticed at once, that light flooded the sector, but a light so bright it dazzled and disorientated, rather than infusing her with a sparkling glow or the warmth brought by sunshine on a hot day in London. She gravitated around the sector, exploring the space. No other energies assembled there, it looked it would be just her and Virder, biding the perfect opportunity to confront him about his deception.

"Ah, young un. You are here. The One informed me you were to join the program and return to the fold."

Sketch pushed a wave of darkness towards Virder, hoping to demonstrate her disapproval at his actions, but watched in awe as he first blocked and then dispersed it into the bright light surrounding them.

"There is always some residual resistance at the start. You'll come to understand the importance of this process," said Virder, his tone calm and steady. *Why is he not thrown by my actions?* Sketch thought.

"First, I need to hear all you think you know about the humans, to understand what truths and which lies you have been fed during your time in their haphazard world."

"I...I don't know where to start," said Sketch in the vibrational equivalent of a mumble.

"Tell me about the boy. Tell me about him."

TWENTY-TWO

London Christmas 1991

LONDON CHRISTMAS 1991

UNLIKE CHRISTMAS DAY 1980, John didn't awake on the twenty-fifth December 1991 until after eleven o'clock. By the time he lumbered down the stairs, Maud had drunk two pots of tea and eaten half a loaf of toasted bread. If he hadn't appeared, then she would have gone into his room and bounced on his bed. He had the better bed for bouncing on and although she wouldn't admit it, for she was far too old for such shenanigans, she sometimes would nip into his room when he was up in the north and have a little bounce.

"Happy Chrimbo, Mum," he said, the lazy grin of a late teenage boy who'd not long awoken from a beer-induced sleep plastered across his face. "What's for breakfast?"

Maud pulled a 'you're kidding me' face and pointed at the clock before walking across to her son and giving him an enormous cuddle. "Merry Christmas little one."

"Does that mean I can have brekkie?" He said, winking at his mum. "It would be a terrible thing if I died of hunger on Christmas Day."

"Of course you can have food. Eat quickly because," before Maud could complete her sentence, John jumped in with what was a traditional refrain.

"You can't open your presents without food in your belly."

"Well, you'd be disappointed if I didn't say it."

As John fixed himself some breakfast, Maud continued onwards with the preparations for dinner. The turkey had been in the oven for a little while and only just fitted the space. She had prepared the majority of the veg the night before but there was bread sauce to be made, Yorkshire pudding batter to be battered and all the sides, nibbles and treats that made the celebratory meal what it was to be sorted.

After John was done scoffing his breakfast, they moved into the small living room and took turns to hand out the gift-wrapped presents from the small piles underneath the tree. The fairy lights have been switched on first thing in the morning, when Maud got up, with the enthusiasm of a small child. Waiting for John to stop being a teenager and wake up had been torturous.

"Open that one first," she said pointing to a large rectangular shaped object wrapped in paper covered in reindeer with red noses and branches of holly.

"I've been wondering what this might be," said John.

"Well, go on then, open it."

John tore off the paper and stood back, staring at his mum with wide eyes and a mouth that didn't seem to be able to get any words to come out of it.

"Mum, a computer! An actual computer. But this is too much."

Maud's eyes twinkled. "I can always take it back to the shop."

"That's not what I mean. Don't take it back to the shop. But, well, it costs such a lot of money."

"I was thinking about your studies. This is going to make it much easier for you. No more having to book into the library to get a slot on one of the University computers now you've got your own. Is it okay? Is it the right type?"

"It's perfect." John continued to stare at the box turning it around and grinning the biggest grin a mother could want to see from her child on Christmas Day.

The present giving bit of the day was over all too soon, although Maud and John had a tradition where they left one present until the evening. While the day wasn't just about gifts, it was part of it that they really loved. Maud busied herself in the kitchen, having the odd sip of brandy, to get everything ready for her guests to arrive. She only stopped when it was time for Top of the Pops. She watched religiously every year with John making commentary on the quality of songs that had hit the charts during the year. This December it included that Bryan Adams song. John hated it, but Maud kind of liked it.

Just before the Queen's speech, there came a knock at the door and John jumped up to answer it. He hadn't caught up with Beverley and her family since returning from university and was keen to see them. Bubbles of noise filled the lower floor of the house as everyone gathered together wishing each other a Merry Christmas and getting settled in for dinner.

After everyone had eaten more food than they could imagine was possible, drank through a number of bottles of wine and beer, the group settled down on the sofa and the spaces on the floor of the living room to watch a film. Aside from the sound of the TV all that could be heard was the rustle of chocolate being unwrapped. Maud caught Beverley's eye and nodded her head towards the door to the kitchen. She arose quietly, tiptoeing out in an attempt not to disturb people relaxing in front of the TV. Beverly followed her to the kitchen.

"Oh Maud, that was such a lovely meal. You make the best Christmas dinner. After all these years in London, I've come to love Christmas. Thank you so much for having us."

"You know you're always welcome. Christmas wouldn't be the same without you. I've got a little something for you," said Maud.

"But you've already given me a present," said Beverley.

"This is just a tiny thing," said Maud. " The thing is, I've also got a favour to ask you but first open your gift." She smiled as she passed Beverley a small square box wrapped in Christmas paper. Beverley turned it around in her hands before carefully peeling off the Sell-otape sticking down the edges of the paper. Maud was always impressed by how meticulous Beverley was at unwrapping gifts and knew she would take the paper home and find a way to reuse it.

"Oh, it's beautiful," said Beverley holding up a thin gold coloured necklace on which hung a pendant in the shape of a daffodil. "My favourite flower."

"I saw it within a pile of junk in a charity shop, and it made me think of you. Now you can have that daffodil feeling whatever the time of year."

"So, what's the favour you want to ask me?"

Maud fished into the drawer at the side of the kitchen and table pulled out a crisp envelope. On it, the date October 2014, was written in precise, ink blue script. The only other word on the paper read Sketch.

I need you to look after this for me. Keep it safe and when the day comes to give it to a young woman called Sketch."

Beverly stared at her quizzically. "Sketch? Who is she? I don't think I know anyone with a name like that."

"I can't explain," said Maud. "All I can tell you is that you will know what to do when the time comes."

TWENTY-THREE

London 2014

MICHAEL MANAGED his frustrations about life by spending time searching for traces of other energies from the Core on the internet. Having the knowledge of who he was had been liberating at first, but, as the unfairness of his situation became apparent and as Clare stopped talking to him about his past existence, he realised that taking action could be the sole way of keeping him from becoming depressed. With the return of his memory had also come access to information about the human world which had been hidden in the recesses of his mind. The part of him that was Inco had woken up, but he still had no one else to speak to about it. After the decades of searching and thinking he'd made Sketch up, finding out she'd been here for months and that he'd missed her by seconds bit into his happiness and left him feeling lonely.

"You still looking for other yous?" asked Clare, bringing in a couple of cups of tea and some biscuits on a flowery plastic tray. "It doesn't seem to be making you feel any better." She stood waiting for his reply. When it didn't come, she placed the mug beside him on a coaster and retreated to the sofa with a book. When he spotted the hot drink perched next to him, Michael turned his head and looked over his shoulder.

"Oh, did you bring this? I didn't hear you come in."

"You were engrossed in the search."

"Sorry, Clare. This is important."

"More important than me?"

He whirled around in his chair. "Of course not, what would make you say something like that?"

Clare's eyes focused on a corner of the sofa which had a purple stain from spilt wine.

"Nothing's more important than you Clare, but I need to know if anyone else is out there, anyone like me." Age had contributed about fifty per cent of grey to his once dark brown hair which followed the pattern of many men's in its receding nature, He noticed it again as he ran his fingers through the fine strands on his head, as was his habit.

"I'm just worried. Now you have all this stuff in your head, and you know where you come from, where you belong, what's to stop you leaving?"

"I've no intention of going anywhere. This is my home, with you." He wheeled his desk chair across to the sofa and bent over and took Clare's hand. "You have to trust me about this."

"So," she started without removing his hand from hers. "So, you're saying if you had a chance to go back to how things were, go back to your life as an energy in the computer, you wouldn't?"

Michael was unsure if this was a question or a statement, so he paused to evaluate her words and to decide how best to reply. He hadn't felt this confused or conflicted since Rebecca, the young women who he'd fallen in love with when he first became a human.

"Well, your silence says it all. I'm not as important as you claim."

"Don't do that. Don't cry, Clare. That's not what I think or feel. You are magicking up words and putting them in my mouth." Clare pulled a crumpled paper tissue from the sleeve of her jumper and blew her nose. He watched the way she did it and then kissed her forehead, knowing this wasn't the right moment for that particular brand of affection but wanting to do it regardless. Her skin was warm and soft as his lips touched it and he has filled once again with awe at the nature of the human physical form and how it contrasted with the freedom of being pure energy. Two divergent ways of existing and he had had the privilege of experiencing them both in one phase of awareness.

"Sorry," said Clare, her words filtered through snot and tears. "I'm scared you'll go back. That you'll go back for her."

"Who?" Michael knew who Clare referred to, but the question seemed necessary to quell the situation and make her feel safe.

"Sketch. You loved her. You said that back in the Core you were close and if that's true and she's gone back, what's to say you can't do that either."

"If I was going to go, I could have done it already."

"Maybe."

"What can I do to convince you that what I say is true?" said Michael, gripping the hand with a growing passion.

"I don't know. None of this is logical. It's just how I feel."

The two sat in silence, holding onto one another and Michael made a decision which tore him in half.

"Let's move away from here. Away from London, from the computer, from Sketch and her friends. We can't do anything to bring her back, and you are right, all the searching online is making me feel worse, not better."

"Really? You'd do that for me?" Clare stared into his eyes. It was one of the ways this life form checked for truth and validity, and so he mirrored her actions and stared back.

"Yes, you are my person. The one for me. My to the moon and back, my soul mate. Whatever you want to call it that's what you are to me."

She pulled him from the swivel chair to the sofa, so he lay on top of her and she kissed him as if they'd first met that night. "I love you," she said as their lips parted.

"I love you too."

"What about the business?" she pushed him away creating a gap of inches between their mouths. "I know work isn't romantic and all, but we will need to eat. None of that 'we'll live on our love' business."

"Ahhh, you can tell you used to work for a bank. We could sell it or get someone to run it for us, or the other option is to start again somewhere else."

"Or a combination of them all. I can talk to my college network online and see what work is going in other areas."

"Perfect."

Michael's mind began to run circles around itself. This solution had stopped Clare from crying, but could he really leave the piece of him which was Inco behind forever?

TWENTY-FOUR

The Core

____

PIX GREETED Sketch on her return from three days in the re-education sector with Virder. Her pulses remained neutral, but by now Sketch understood how to interpret them. Virder, under the guise of manipulating Sketch into being a puppet of the One, had instructed her the ways of the Resistance. Being unable to decode messages transmitted from energy to energy was just one of the vital pieces of information he'd shared with her. She loved the secret knowledge and being part of something so important, and she was excited to now be able to communicate with Pix.

The code used by the Resistance wasn't detected by the One or any of the energies in his circle, because it had been adopted by a primitive means of communication once used by the humans. Morse code consisted of a series of short and long pulses of light. Each set represented a letter of the alphabet used by many humans on the western side of the globe to form words. It was invented in the 1800s by one of the inventors of the telegraph. Sketch thought it to be the most perfect fit for energies and one in which they could communicate without fear of being discovered. The One and his cronies expected more sophisticated methods of subterfuge.

Sketch's first Morse to Pix allowed her to be herself once more, although she was careful to remain in control of her aura and its tendency to spew out sparks of light when she became excited or enthused.

- Pix, I am most happy to be friends you! Virder has told me much about how you have helped in the battle to take back the Core.

- And I have waited a long time to talk with you, Sketch. I worried you would be taken in by the One. Perhaps I shouldn't have encouraged you to return here.

- You? It was you who helped me get back? Oh!

- I could see you wanted to be back with us, but the One encouraged us to stay dark until he was ready for us to let the human users know the computer could be operated again.

- So, the light? That was you?

- With the help of Virder, I managed to send out enough light for you to know we were still in existence. That a return was possible.

Pix's aura dimmed to a level indicating to Sketch that there was something her new friend hadn't yet told her.

- What is it Pix?

- We didn't tell you about your friends. About Inco, about the One, about all the other energies you thought you were returning to. We should have told you, but I thought you might not come back if you knew.

- And you needed me? You needed me to join the Resistance?

- Yes. Are you mad at me? I'd understand if you don't want to Morse with me.

Sketch desired to wrap Pix with a blanket of nourishing light.

- Don't be daft, as the humans say. I am most pleased to have a friend again. Someone to talk to or Morse with.

- But would you have returned if you'd known the truth?

She stopped to think. Would she have?

- I'm not sure. Being a human can be very confusing. I kissed a boy. He kissed me back and then he changed his mind and then and there I just wanted to come home. If I'd realised Inco was the human called Michael that may have changed my mind. But what I do know is that I would have wanted to help whether it be from this side or that.

- Sketch, you are an energy to surpass all energies.

Had she had human form, Sketch would have laughed out loud, lolled at Pix's comment. It wasn't so long ago, she'd been a failing trainee energy sent to the human world because she was making such a shambles of her role.

- And you are an inspiration to me, Pix. Pix?

- Yes, Sketch.

- Do you miss twirling and sparking and making your aura as bright as it can possibly go?

- So much. You can't even imagine how much. To spark and twirl is the best thing ever.

- Sparking and twirling is pretty amazing but then you've never kissed a human boy!

- Or a human girl. Do you think that's as good?

- I think kissing should be wonderful whether the human is male or female. Kissing is all lips, tongues, chemistry and sparks.

- Ohhhh and we're the experts at sparks!

Something which had been missing in Sketch's life in the Core was back. She had a friend again.

As their work period drew to a close and they were preparing to hand over their duties to an alternate set of energies, their zone became flooded with a darkness. It could only signify something unusual was about to occur, but whether it transpired to be positive or negative, Sketch couldn't tell. She stopped herself from Morsing to Pix in case of ensuing danger, but her friend continued to send out coded light signals in her direction.

"This work zone is under investigation. All energies will stay static in their positions until questioning is complete. Do not attempt to pulse to one another. Do not communicate in any way with the inquisitors, unless they first speak to you. Failure to adhere to these instructions will result in immediate recycling. There will be no exceptions."

A wave of panic shot through Sketch's being, but she moderated herself remembering Virder had told her such investigations were a matter of routine. She had no reason to suspect they had uncovered her part in the Resistance. Instead, she focused on presenting the appearance of the most compliant and loyal energy within the zone. When the investigator presented itself to her, she was ready to play one of the most important parts of her existence.

TWENTY-FIVE

London 2001

A LONG-HAIRED, black cat sauntered up the road and rubbed itself against Maud's legs.

"Hello, little one. Where did you come from?" She bent down and stroked the cat. "You're a cute one." Maud continued on towards home, and the cat scurried along beside her as if they were friends. A sonorous purr came from within the feline, followed by a short meow.

"What a shame I don't talk kitty. I suppose I could try, but then I'd have no idea what I'd be saying." As if in response, the cat moved closer and rubbed its face around her legs, twisting in and out.

"Careful now. You'll be tripping me up, and I don't want to be laid up. My family is coming around tomorrow. Martin, my grandson, is as cute as, well, as cute as you." Maud wondered at the way the cat avoided oncoming pedestrians and their plastic bags, children and wheelie suitcases. Felines were smart or at least this one was.

They turned off into Maud's street. The cat strolled with the confidence of someone who knew where they were going which made it a funny fluffy little thing in Maud's mind. On reaching her front door, the cat showed no sign of disappearing, instead recommencing its twirling around Maud's legs accompanied by rapid meowing.

"Are you hungry, little one? I suppose there might be something in the fridge you could eat. You can't come in but stay here, and I'll be right back."

The cat continued to talk in meows as Maud unlocked the door and entered her house, at pains to keep the cat outside. As gorgeous as it looked and as hungry as it sounded an animal would make a mess of the house which she prided herself in keeping spick and span. True to her word, Maud rescued some left-over chicken from the fridge. She'd earmarked it for making soup, but there'd be enough for both of them. She chopped it up into small pieces hoping they would be suitable for a cat to eat. She wasn't sure what cats ate, but she did know she didn't have any mice in the freezer.

On opening the front door, Maud found the cat still there sitting on its hind legs and waiting with what would have looked like a smile, but she knew cats didn't grin except on cartoons or in stories about girls called Alice. The kitty tore into the chicken with relish, leaving Maud pleased she'd done a nice thing for the animal.

It was an hour or so later when she heard the expected knock on the door heralding the anticipated arrival of her family. A visit from John, Sarah and Martin sat high on her list of favourite bits of the week. She'd made some of her delicious cheese scones and John's favoured shortbread and bought in some bottles of the fizzy pop her grandson liked, even though his parents weren't keen on him drinking it.

"Hello mum," said John as she let them in through the front door. He kissed her on the cheek. "Looks like you've got a new friend." He pointed towards the long-haired cat who Martin was playing with.

"Grannie Maud, can Clock come in?" He said with a smile she found it easy to give in to.

"Who's Clock when he's at home?"

"The cat of course."

Maud looked at her grandson with a sense of awe at his confidence. Small children didn't seem to feel fear or have the same filters as adults.

"He's not our cat, so he has to stay outside."

"But Grannie."

Sarah took hold of his small hand which wasn't stroking the cat and tugged him away. "If Grannie Maud says no, she's saying it for a reason. It's a beautiful cat, and he's probably got a home to be getting back to."

"But Clock says she hasn't got a home."

"Now you're just being silly," said Sarah. "Go on, get inside in the warm."

Maud noticed how sad and grumpy Martin looked and thought it odd how he had become so attached to the cat in such a short period.

"It was very nice of you to give the kitty a name. How do you know the cat is a girl cat?"

"Because she told me of course. She told me her name too."

The adults laughed at looked from one another. *He really is the cutest grandson I could have*, thought Maud. She hated to see him down in the dumps and his eyes welling up with tears.

"Oh, go on then. The cat."

"Clock," said Martin straight-faced to his grandmother.

"Yes, of course. Silly me. Clock can come inside for a little bit."

Martin grabbed his grannie's legs and hugged them, then turned to Clock. "Did you hear that, Clock? You'll be one of the family now."

Maud began to protest and then wondered if he could be right. The cat had followed her home and become instant best friends with Martin, so maybe she should think about what the child was saying, even though she didn't fancy having a pet.

That afternoon, all Martin's attention focused on Clock the cat. They played and chattered and lay on the carpet face-to-face, Martin giggling when Clock licked his nose.

"Cat kisses," said John watching from the sofa.

"That's not hygienic," said Sarah, grabbing a wet wipe from her bag.

"It'll do him no harm," said John. "Cats are very clean creatures. I saw it on a documentary." He turned to Maud. "We've got something we want to talk to you about."

Maud saw a tell-tale wrinkle appear on John's forehead. He'd had it from childhood, and it became noticeable when he was worried about saying something to her.

"What's wrong?"

"It's not so much that something is wrong. I've been offered a job. It'd be a promotion and so much more interesting than what I'm doing now."

"But..." said Maud seeing the downside coming.

"But the job is in Australia."

TWENTY-SIX

London 2014

SINCE SKETCH HAD LEFT life in London, Matt found himself spending more and more time with Ashling and Sammy and found himself enjoying it. Having taken him some time to get used to the idea of being a teenage dad and having a small child and his mother living with him, he described himself as coming late to the party. But now he regretted not having been around in the early days and missing Sammy's first steps, words and other baby to child milestones parents find essential.

"Don't you think things seem weird without Sketch?" asked Ashling as they walked back from toddler soft play at the community centre. "I miss the way she looks at the world, even if it could be way too positive at times.

"Yeh, I know what you mean. I find myself thinking, 'What would Sketch say?' But my version isn't half as good as hers would be."

"Sketch," said Sammy spinning around.

"I remember her teaching him to do that," said Ashling. Matt thought he might melt as his mind and body leapt back in time to the physical memory of his brief kiss with Sketch.

"Matt, earth calling Matt." Ashling's words and her hand waving in front of his nose brought him back.

"There you are. You had that wistful look on your face. You once had that with me, and that resulted in Sammy. Was there something going on with you and Sketch?"

He avoided catching Ashling's eye as he fiddled with one of Sammy's toy plastic diggers. "Nah, she's like my sister. That be weird."

"You're not convincing anyone Matt! Don't forget I've got the best bullshit radar when it comes to you. It's honed by experience."

Matt pulled an anguished face. "Ok, you don't have to rub it in. I was wrong. Past. Bygones and all that."

"Sketch always liked you. She fell apart, albeit for a few hours, when you got together with Britney at that party. That's why she was so upset when that moron Harry did the same."

Matt put the digger down. "I'm not like him. Ok, so I might have kissed her."

"All the OMGness Matt. You kissed Sketch? I mean, I was fishing, but I never imagined anything had happened. Why didn't you say something?"

"Because it's my fault she went there. Back to the Core, I mean."

"How can you think you are to blame? Sketch had been trying to get back to the Core for months. All that stuff at school, gardening, Harry it was all just a filler until the computer was fixed."

"It is. You don't understand."

"No, I don't understand. You're right. Perhaps you could tell me." Matt was reluctant to share. Ashling had been quick to judge him in the past so that was very reason she wouldn't do the same now. But she was right. He had a terrible track record and been awful to her about Sammy.

"Tell me, Matt."

He shuffled on his seat, wanting more than ever not to have started this strand of the conversation. He used to have a blog which he used to share his thoughts with the world anonymously. Perhaps now was a good time to bring it back but that wouldn't solve his current problem. Looking at Ashling's face, he realised she wasn't going to give up until he told her what was causing him the angst.

He sighed. "Well, after we kissed, it was a good kiss, in fact, it was an amazing kiss, but then I freaked out. I got scared, and I told her it wasn't right, that I couldn't do it. And the look on her face, Ash." He looked up to check Ashling's reaction. He was surprised to see her looking sympathetic.

"Go on," she said.

"I think I broke her. I think it was me. It happened the night she went back to the Core, and I realised too late how much I cared about her."

"You can be such a dufus sometimes Matt, but I'm sure that's not the reason she went back. More like it was awful timing. The thing with the kiss, it could have happened at any point, but it was a coincidence that the computer spurted back to life the same night."

"I still think it's because of me."

"Whatever. I guess I can't convince you otherwise, but I can give you a hug. Come here dufus."

Unhugged for too long, Matt melted into Ashling's embrace, feeling at once comforted by the touch of another being even though it wasn't the one he wished for. The hug lasted a second or two longer than either one of them was comfortable with, soon pulling away, Matt became awkward and aware of the gangly nature of his body. It didn't live up to the expectations he had as to what it should look like, but he didn't have the inclination to go to the gym.

"Errr, Thanks, Ash."

"She still might come back you know. It's not a done deal, but."

"There's always a but."

"Life is full of them. And as I was saying, you can't put your life on hold on the off chance." He knew what she was saying made sense, but he couldn't give up on Sketch, not yet.

"Yeh, so what do you think about this Michael guy? Strange him popping up and announcing he's from the computer just after Sketch left."

"He seems okay to me. I mean it must be mega weird if what he says is true."

"You think he's lying?"

"No. Why would he? And if we believe Sketch."

"Which we do. Then we have to believe him too."

As they talked Sammy piled up bricks and moved them around the handle of his digger oblivious to the conversation his parents were having.

"Mummy, Sammy watch Duggee?" And they turned back to childcare and kids TV.

TWENTY-SEVEN

The Core

AS EXPECTED BY SKETCH, the investigation team underwent a spot check of her work station. Each area was examined for unexpected energy traces which might indicate the presence of someone who shouldn't have been there or for inappropriate behaviour as defined by the One. The investigators also took each of the workers aside, one-by-one to interrogate them about their routine with each energy being given a firm steer to report any unexpected activity to the investigators. Sketch knew she was safe with Pix. Her fellow Resistance member could hold her own and not betray herself or others, and Sketch was confident the energy had the wherewithal to put on an expert display of neutrality. The other energies in their workstation zone were an unknown quantity. None of them had participated in the Morsing conversations, nor had they showed an interest in anything Sketch was doing. However, this didn't mean they weren't observing her, keeping track of her actions so as to report back to the One or his team of investigators. But given that this was beyond Sketch's control, she decided to concentrate on running through the answers to the questions she expected them to put to her.

Just two other energies remained unquestioned when Sketch was summoned by the officials. Pix and the others had been dispensed of and sent to a section of the zone to await the completion of the investigation. Sketch quivered, her bravery abandoning her as she realised the extent of the danger she found herself in. Not for the first time, she longed for Inco, for Jackie, Maud, Matt, Trevor or sausages; all which were impossible for her to have.

"You are allotted to this work station?"

"Yes, investigator," said Sketch, lowering her aura in deference to their status. There had always been a hierarchy in the Core, but the extent of the current structure galled her.

"Have you deviated from your tasks during the last period?"

"No."

"No, what?"

"Oh sorry, no, investigator. Sorry, you are making me a little nervous. Please forgive my omission."

The investigator continued without acknowledging her apology. "I can confirm your tasks have been completed with expediency. Are you aware of any deviations performed by other energies in your zone?"

The question unnerved Sketch. It wasn't one from the list of regular queries Virder had shared with her, and she had no prepared answer other than the obvious.

"No, Investigator."

The energy appeared satisfied, but Sketch experienced a ripple of discomfort through her power source akin to a chill.

"Are you of certainty about my last question?"

"Affirmative, Investigator Sir. I've not seen anything strange or outside of the parameters of the role of those stationed in this zone."

"You may disperse and join the other approved workers."

The chill stayed with her as she made her way to join Pix and the others. She sensed the unexpected investigation was anything but routine. Gravitating towards Pix for the safety and comfort of an ally, Sketch struggled to maintain her togetherness. The lying, deception and mistruths were things which didn't came easily to her. She'd not had much practice at it. Despite Morsing being a disguised form of communication, there was an implicit agreement between the two resistance members not to use it in the vicinity of the investigators, better to wait than risk being discovered and throwing the operation into jeopardy.

Time slowed as the final energies were interrogated by the Investigators. Both Pix and Sketch fidgeted as if they had a gang of ants in their pants; finding it tricky to remain still and unagitated.

The final energy arrived in their holding location, allowing them to fluctuate their auras a little. As they began to return to a state of normality, the investigators swooped in, bringing with them their characteristic cloak of light reduction. The group steadied itself.

"The energy labelled Pix is required to accompany us to the One for further questioning."

Sketch baulked on hearing this command and failed to prevent a series of Morse pulses making their way in the direction of Pix.

- Stay strong. It will be ok. I'll tell Virder.

But Pix didn't acknowledge receipt of them or indicate in any way that she was perturbed by the order to report to their leader. As she was led away by the investigators, the energies returned to their non-work positions allowing the next shift of workers to take over. Sketch regressed to worrying about her new friend and how the energy might be treated under interrogation by the One. Pix was one of the most together energies Sketch had encountered so she hoped the entity would be fine but what if the investigators had discovered something of interest to the One? In such circumstances, Pix's existence and those of members of the Resistance might be in peril. But there was nothing Sketch could do other than to inform Virder. In order to do so, she was required to contact via Morse the next energy in the communication line from Pix. This system operated a like a human telephone tree from before the time of mobile phones and internet-based messaging. One energy passed a message to another and so on until it reached its pre-ordained recipient. Sketch moderated her aura, attempting to appear inconspicuous as she travelled to the next zone in the Core. On arrival, she paused and surveyed her surroundings until she located the energy she wished to communicate with. When stationed in their proximity, Sketch began to Morse.

- Pix has been brought in by the investigators. Please pass a message to Virder. This is urgent.

Sketch waited for a response which came quickly.

- I understand. Affirmative. The message will be transmitted. Please attend to your zone.

She followed the instructions until she located herself back in her non-work station, but without Pix she was alone with no one to talk to, no one to Morse with and no opportunity to sparkle or spiral. All she could do was stay still and wait, and waiting was something Sketch wasn't adept at. She exhaled a small amount of light in the shape of what she imagined a sigh would look like.

TWENTY-EIGHT

London 2005

OF ALL THE constants of her life in London, the local library was one of her favourites making Maud both a regular visitor and a regular reader. She enjoyed keeping up with current affairs but also getting other people's view of the world expressed through novels and poetry and plays. Many of the books available on the shelves changed, rotating through the different libraries of the borough. The window displays aimed at encouraging people to pop in, borrow books and enjoy reading also switched with the seasons, like a calendar marking time over the years.

As well a churn in books and furniture the staff came and went. Maud made an effort to get to know each of them because they were the experts in their field and had the power to point her towards knowledge and stories to aid her in escaping the everyday. Although she liked all of them, Maud was keen to make the acquaintance of a new young librarian, fresh from college and sporting a very straight fringe. Aside from her hair young, the woman stood out because of her unusual name, Begw, and her North Waleian accent.

"Welcome to our little library," said Maud when introduced to Begw. "I have a strong feeling you're going to like it here."

"Do you think? This is just a temporary, for six months. Then I'm thinking about moving on."

"That's the thing with young people," said Maud. "Always got your head in tomorrow. That's not a bad thing, but I bet you my pension; you'll still be here in five years." Begw snorted and smiled at Maud.

"We'll see. Though I'm not sure about taking your pension from you." The pair discussed the latest novels to arrive on the metal shelves of the library's numerous bookcases, the new electronic system for checking in and out your books and the lack of date stamps that went with it.

"I like to see the dates. There's something about the history of the books that come from seeing how many times it's been taken out, and I like to imagine the people who've thumbed through the pages. It's harder to imagine who they might be without those date stamps."

"Me too," agreed Begw. "There's too much new technology taking over. Give me an electric typewriter, a memo and some cardboard library cards, and I'll be in heaven."

The forthright nature of Begw made Maud chortle. "I like the idea of technology if I'm honest, but I'm a bit scared by it. Can't be doing with all these computers and shiny phones. As long as I've got books, I'm happy."

"You're a woman after my own heart, Maud. I think we are going to get on really well."

"Now, can you order some books for me? My church book group is keen to read the latest Harry Potter novel."

"Oh, everyone is after that, but let me see what I can do for you. While you're there can I ask you something?"

"Ask away," said Maud undoing the buttons on her favourite purple coat.

"Can I get you a panad?"

Maud looked back at the woman and raised her eyebrows. "I'd love a cuppa, thank you. Milk and two sugars please."

"Do you speak Welsh?" Begw grinned.

"A smattering of words here and there. Picked them up in a

book of poems. I'll try to remember to dig it out for you. I think you'd enjoy it."

"Why, thanks very much. Love a good poem me." Begw excused herself to make the drinks and Maud wandered over to look at the day's newspapers. Much of the papers concerned themselves with the upcoming general election, but that wasn't what interested Maud. She always flipped first to the business pages and the sections where technological breakthroughs were mentioned. This year had already seen the invention of an online map program called Google Maps. What most fascinated Maud was the speed of change. Once the humans started something, they didn't mess about. It wouldn't be long before people would be wired into the internet of everything by a small DNA disrupting chip which released chemicals designed to speed up the evolution of humans, but Maud wouldn't be around to witness this transformation.

Begw returned with two steaming mugs of tea and sat them on the vinyl-topped table.

"Now Maud, I've been making a plan, and I want your input. If you could have the perfect library what would it look like?"

Maud pondered Begw's question for she wasn't sure what a perfect library would look like and if her vision would work for anyone else. She attempted to carve an answer with her human head on.

"If I had a wish list it would go like this: 1. All kinds of people of different ages would visit the library because it had opening hours which fitted with people's work and life patterns. People would be able to drop in on evenings and Sundays when they're not at work. 2. It would have talks by authors, local authors and some-times people who've written bestsellers because people who write books are just people. 3. It would be wonderful to have an area where you could have a cuppa and have a natter. The rest of the library can be quiet but having a space to talk to others about books and everyday nonsense is important too. 4. More classes for people like me who look like we know everything but don't." Maud winked at Begw as she made her last point and the librarian scribbled down notes.

"That's very helpful. We can't do anything until we find more funding when we do this will help. Your vision matches with mine. You have a good mind, Maud."

She raised up her mug and clinked it against Maud's. "To the library."

"To the library."

TWENTY-NINE

London 2014

MAE WONDERED if Jackie had slipped something into her tea because it was either that or the woman had lost the plot. She pushed the half drink cup across the table just in case it had caused some kind of psychotic episode. What was she supposed to say to some woman who told her Sketch had gone to live inside of a computer? The whole thing was mental as.

"I think I better go," she said. "My Grandma's expecting me." She began to rise from the wooden chair when Jackie took her by the hand.

"It would be strange if you didn't think I was a bit bonkers," said Jackie. "God knows, there are times when I doubt my own sanity, but I promise you what I'm telling you is the truth."

Mae stared at her, checking out body language, eye movement and facial expressions. The thing was this Jackie looked in every way like she was being honest. "Prove it then."

"It's not that easy."

"Course it's not. You sound like a nice person and Sketch, well she said good things about you, but this, well, this is too much." Mae pulled her hand away. "I'm sorry. Gotta go." Before she got to the stairs, she turned and saw Jackie with her head on the table, her hands entwined in her hair. Should she stay and attempt to help her? She wanted to but didn't know what to do or say so turned back to climb the stairs and leave the house.

"Wait." Jackie's voice halted her steps. "You said you had something for Sketch. What is it?"

Mae fingered the letter, its cover thinned by the decades of exposure to the stale air of Beverley's sideboard drawer. She turned back and extracted it from her pocket.

"A letter. She said she'd promised someone called Maud she'd give it to Sketch. Dunno what this is all about. She never even met Sketch. I just told her about my friends at the college and how much fun Sketch was. She's not all there anymore, my Grandma." Mae's eyes began to fill with tears. "You can't give it to her though can you? Even if she's not in a computer, you can't get it to her."

Jackie shook her head. "No, I can't. Can I see it?"

"It's just for Sketch. I promised Grandma I'd give it to Sketch and she promised this Maud the same."

"I knew Maud. She and Sketch were friends."

Mae stepped closer to Jackie. "Were?"

"Maud died last year."

"So, some dead lady wrote a letter for Sketch and gave it to my Grandma to give her now. That's doesn't make any sense."

"No, it doesn't. Look, Mae, I know you don't believe me about Sketch, about her true identity but I think we should read the letter. It might hold some clue as to how we can help.'

"I dunno. The envelope says Sketch. Grandma insisted it go to Sketch."

"What about if we steam it open? If there's nothing to worry about we can reseal it then and Sketch will never know we've opened it. But..."

"...if there's something bad in it we'll know?"

"Yes."

The pair examined each other, speaking with the language of their eyes rather than relying on words. Mae bit her lip. Jackie rubbed her arms.

"Put the kettle on again, then." Mae took the envelope and placed it in the middle of the table. She stood watching it as if its contents had the power to come alive. Time shifted, making the kettle appear to take longer than usual to fill, giving more time for Mae to wonder if she'd made the right decision about the letter.

As soon as the kettle clicked off Jackie brought it from the kitchen to the table.

"Are you ready?" she asked. Mae nodded. She wasn't sure this was the right thing to do, but after the strange conversation and her Grandma's insistence, it now seemed vital to know the contents of the letter. She took the envelope and held it close to the steam, trying not to burn herself with the vaporised water.

"It always looks much easier to do this on the telly," she said.

Jackie gave a little laugh, tinged with nervousness. "Most things do. If you turn it around a bit, it will get all of the seal."

Mae turned the faded envelope from side-to-side, flicking her eyes between the paper and Jackie until the latter gestured for her to stop. She placed it in front of her and with a subtle nod from Jackie began to gently peel the top paper triangle from its counterpart below. Careful not to damage the envelope, she took her time and held her breath as she worked. As the flap opened, she allowed herself to exhale and saw Jackie do the same.

"Shall I read it?" she asked.

Jackie nodded. "Yes, go on."

"I'm not sure I can. This is too weird."

"Give it a go, and if not I can help."

With shaking fingers, Mae prised a number of pieces of ruled paper from the envelope. Below an address in Camden was written the year 1991. What? How could this letter have been written over fifteen years ago?

"What does it say?" asked Jackie.

"It's old, innit. Hang on, and I'll read it out." Mae sat up straight as if giving a performance and began to speak.

"'Dear Sketch,

By the time you get this letter we will have met in the human world, but I will be gone.' What does she mean by 'the human world'?" asked Mae.

"Like I told you," said Jackie. "Sketch isn't from our world, but I've no idea how Maud knew that. She was just an old lady who went to Sketch's class at the library. I mean, Sketch loved her, but I'm sure she wouldn't have let her in on her secret. Keep going."

THIRTY

The Core

———————

TWO WORK SHIFT patterns went by with no news of Pix, although another energy replaced her at the work station. No word came back from Virder or from any of the other energies. Sketch's aura bounced between convincing herself everything was fine and imagining a range of worst case scenarios. *I have to stop this,* she thought. Dreaming up thoughts of Pix being transformed into a stick insect, a piece of metal rail track or a grain of sand buffeted around by salty tides wasn't doing her any good. But what in the human realm has happened to Virder? Why hadn't he replied to her emergency morse? It struck her the questions were mounting up, and she might have to find the answers by herself. Perhaps she should request an audience with the One but would require a reason, a justification for taking up his time.

As she pondered the best excuse to make, she became aware of a new energy in the zone. It was outside her work period, so interaction was permissible though not encouraged. Not in the way it had been during her previous time in the Core when she took every opportunity to hang out with Inco.

The reason for the new arrival became apparent as their aura began to emit Morse pulses. Sketch switched her interpretive function to understand this other language.

- I bring grim tidings of ill will. Virder and many other members of the Resistance have been detained by the One's investigators.

-What? morsed Sketch.

- This is the message I have been tasked to transmit.

- Who is the next recipient?

- There are no further recipients. You are the final destination for the message.

The Resistance energy's aura flexed in a shrug.

- Is that all there is? Is there no more?

- No, that is it. You are one of five free members of the resistance and have ultimate decision-making power. Oh, and I was told to tell you resistance is anything but futile.

Before Sketch could react or respond to the energy, they dispersed. This proved to be disturbing. She had no idea what she was supposed to do next or the extent of the ultimate decision-making power and who she could contact to bring together the four remaining resistance members. The quandary rolled around her mind. There was a danger she would get lost in all the thinking. But she remembered similar times as a human when she had spent much time thinking too much and not talking to people or doing anything. This time would be different. Sketch was fuelled by a wave of anger, a logical rage. She couldn't just stand back and let this happen. It was up to her. She was going to make the difference, she was going to help her friends escape and, in the process, make contact with the human world and her allies there.

Sketch remembered a snippet of knowledge Virder had told her. At times it was possible to trace the remnants of an energy's aura back to its location. The traces would disappear quickly, so it was important to act before they vanished, like a trail of breadcrumbs through the forest. Sketch settled her mind and zoomed in to the aura of the energy who had passed the morse message to her. It took some time for her to pick up the trace but the sparks where there and the more she focused, the brighter and easier to follow they became. Checking she wouldn't be missed, Sketch began to follow the winding route towards her fellow resistance member's trail. No doubt the energy she was following was attempting to make it difficult to be found, not by Sketch but by the investigators or the One. Sketch kind of enjoyed the subterfuge. She imagined herself as Sketch the undercover agent, hot in pursuit of the only person who could lead her to the truth, someone with that vital clue which would solve the whole crime. After curving around ducking out of sight taking alternate routes not to be seen by the other energies who might be spies, Sketch arrived at a place of light and located the remaining members of the Resistance.

She morsed for them to gather round to share her plan. The plan which had taken shape on her journey to the gathering.

- This is terrible news. It is. But we need to do everything we can to rescue Virder, Pix and the rest of the energies the One has detained. To do this, I need to convince the One that he can trust me. This is going to sound weird, but I intend to tell him everything I know about the Resistance. This way he'll have no reason not to believe me. I will, of course, recommend that he continues to detain our friends, but once he thinks I'm on his side I'll be able to access sectors of the Core which will allow me to reach out to my human friends. With their assistance, we can reverse this tyrannical situation and release the captive energies.

- Do you really think it will work? Piped up one of the energies.

- There are no guarantees, but what alternative do we have? Leaving them where they are isn't an option, and there are not enough of us to try anything else.

- What about us? Do you intend to tell the One about us? Will we be detained as well?

- No. I am relying on you to stay vigilant and cause a distraction if necessary. You must also encourage others to join the resistance if I do not return. This isn't just about me, it isn't just about you, it's about the whole future of life in the Core.

The gathered energies moved closer together joining their auras and experienced the strength of one another. It was a moment of solidarity, and one Sketch vowed to remember as she went about her impossible mission.

THIRTY-ONE

London 2013

———————

ON A SUNDAY in the autumn of 2013, Maud put on her purple coat with the fur trim and examined her reflection in the mirror. She didn't look bad for all the human years her body had lived for, and she still recognised the twinkle in her eye which appeared whenever she smiled. Before leaving the house, she glanced around, knowing the end was about to begin. On the sideboard sat an assortment of photographs, each housed in a frame of wood, brushed metal or shiny plastic. Her eye was drawn to a busy picture of her family her friend Beverley's taken in the early nineties on Christmas day. It hadn't snowed, that wouldn't have been the British way, but they celebrated with joy, singing and a feast of food and drink and some rubbish on the TV. Next to it, encased in a large silver frame was her favourite photograph. She picked up the picture and blew a kiss to its two-dimensional inhabitants, her son John, his wife Sarah and her beautiful grandson Martin. With them on the other side of the world, she never stopped missing them, but at this moment, it hurt more than ever before because she knew she would never see them again.

"I wish you all the best life. Know that I love you." She placed the picture back in its allotted space and buttoned up her coat.

The events of the day were pre-destined, and Maud understood there was little point trying to do anything different. It wouldn't be fair on Sketch, so she set out to the shops. She pulled her empty shopping trolley with her and made her way down the road to the supermarket. On the list were the basics; eggs, milk, bread and some items she rarely bought but loved. For most people, these types of treats would include chocolate, crisps or alcohol but in Maud's case, it was unfashionable things in tins. In the shop, she attached her trolley to the supermarket one and steered them both straight to the aisle with the tinned beans and alike. She set about finding beans and sausages, spaghetti hoops and alphabet spaghetti. Moving down the aisle, she added corned beef and spam to the collection of groceries. She grinned then manoeuvred both trollies towards the newspapers and books, picking a paperback that would take no longer than a few weeks to read. Although still a regular visitor to the library, nothing gave Maud more pleasure than purchasing a book of her own once a month.

A glance at her watch, a gift from John and the family, shipped from Australia, told her it was time to get the tube. Her blood pounded through her body at an excessive speed. This was the first page of the final chapter for Maud but the start of a new book for Sketch.

The Northern line tube pulled into Kentish Town tube station. Maud arose pulling at her shopping trolley full of groceries which snagged itself on the corner of the end seat of the carriage. She managed to free it before the train doors closed, and it pulled off again but struggled to lift it to the platform. Looking up she was assisted by a woman in her early forties with a young woman with spikey blonde hair and piercing green eyes.

"Thank you," said Maud, knowing she'd be seeing Sketch again soon and at last experiencing the comfort of not being the only one of her kind living a life in the human world. As the pair pulled off, she heard their words.

"Poor soul. I can't imagine being that age, doing your weekly."

As the carriage door closed, Maud smiled. Sketch did make a spectacular young human. "Hello, Sketch," she said to the underground train as it pulled off in the direction of Tufnell Park and High Barnet.

On returning home, Maud put her shopping away into the regimented cupboards, leaving out a tin of alphabetti spaghetti for her evening meal. It was fun to make words and then eat them. From a pile of papers on her kitchen table, Maud pulled her most recent journal and began to construct a list of events and actions which would take place over the coming weeks. Without this aide memoire, Maud worried she might forget one of the crucial events needed to keep everything on track. Having already signed up for the Silver Surfers class at the library, the one which Sketch would be teaching, Maud was able to place a giant tick in purple felt-tip pen next to that.

From the cupboard in the sideboard, she removed a half-drunk bottle of brandy. It was time for a toast. She poured herself a generous glass and settled down on the sofa.

"Here's to you, Sketch. May your adventures continue after I'm gone. May your life be fulfilling, and may you never return to the Core for it is no longer there."

She wondered if sending out Sketch on her own to the human world had been the correct thing to do. At the time she considered it expedient to force the fledgling computer energy into a situation where she had no choice but to learn, but now Maud thought that it might have been better for the trainee energy to have been dispersed along with all the other energies. Had the early transformation of Sketch led to the collapse of the Core? They might never know, but Maud's role now was to make sure Sketch felt at home and settled in the human world. It would make it easier for Sketch to adapt when she became stuck in human form forever. There was much to enjoy as a member of the physical world. Love and other emotions, the ability to grow and nourish another person and the beauty of the entire planet to explore. Yes, Sketch could do marvellous things and live a glorious life.

THIRTY-TWO

London 2014

MICHAEL ARRIVED BACK from the shop with a packet of biscuits and a pint of semi-skimmed milk. He found Clare trawling the many property websites of the internet for places they might move to. They'd set criteria including semi-rural with excellent transport links to entertainment and shopping, enough options for building up a new branch of the business and access to super-fast broadband from a cable company. Aside from this, they figured they could make a tidy sum from selling their London home and have a buffer for settling in a new area. Clare had expressed a preference for somewhere by the sea. Her current favourite location being a small Victorian town in the North East called Saltburn by the Sea.

"Hey," she said to Michael touching his arm as he walked past to put the shopping in the kitchen. "Come and look at this one. It's cheap as chips but needs some renovation. It'd be a project we could work on together."

He peered over her shoulder and kissed her on the head reflecting how her hair smelt of honey and how much better it was now they were back on track. Giving up the idea of tracing his fellow Core energies remained challenging for him but still a worthwhile sacrifice to save his relationship with Clare.

"Oh, another one on a jewel street," he said.

"I know you like them."

The Victorian terraces leading down to the cliff tops had piqued Michael's interest because of their names, each of them called after a precious stone such as diamond, ruby and emerald. They'd read that you could hear the rhythmic lapping and lashing of the waves on the shore from inside each house and it sounded to Michael somewhere he might lose himself and find the peace which had eluded him for most of his human life.

"Will there be enough work for us? I know we'll have some money from the business here even taking on a manager, but it won't be enough long-term."

Clare tipped her head up to look at him, and he revelled in her smile. "Well, that's the good news. While you've been out, I've run a search on jobs, parks, gardening and education and I've found a couple of prime opportunities which will suit us both."

She picked up a notebook from next to the keyboard, and he read through her curvy, handwritten list. It included gardeners for the local Italian gardens and a group of big houses on the nearby Yorkshire moors who were looking to employ people to take care of what appeared to be extensive grounds.

"Looks like we're going to do this," he said in more of a statement than a question. "What should we do first? Apply for jobs or look at houses?"

"Let's look at the vacancies but also book in a visit to Teesside to look at the houses we like. What's the harm in having a look?" She turned around and pulled him by the jumper, drawing him into her for a cuddle. As they hugged, Clare's phone vibrated on the desk behind them. Michael held her tight not wanting the closeness to be ended by an electronic device which would herald a further interruption. He wanted Clare all for himself in a bubble of the here and now, but the buzzing of the phone on the hard surface continued. Feeling her discomfort at not answering it, he released his hold and let the air flow between their bodies.

"It's Jackie," said Clare, pressing the green button on the screen and holding the phone to her right ear. "Hello."

As she spoke, Michael watched her. He examined her body language and the expression of her face shift, and her muscles become tense as the conversation continued.

"And where did you say this letter came from?" asked Clare. "Yes, I'll tell him, but we'll need to see it." The conversation paused for seconds allowing the muffled voice of Jackie on the other end of the phone to finish talking.

"Okay, will be over in about an hour. Don't tell anyone else yet. Michael needs to see it first." She turned back to her husband. "I don't know how to say this, so I'm just going to do the best I can. Some friend of Sketch has delivered a letter to Jackie. It was written by someone called Maud who claims to be an energy from your world." Michael's mind began to spiral, and darkness descended as the colour drained from his face and the power keeping him conscious faded away. Michael fell on the sofa leaving Clare aghast. "Michael! Michael wake up. Please be okay." She shook him gently by the shoulders, tears tumbling down her cheeks. Her panicked brain ran through a range of options including phoning 999 to call an ambulance and kissing him on the lips as to wake him from a fairytale slumber. Fortunately, Michael's sleep was short--lived and he began to rouse and gently move bits of his body with his eyes screwed up as his face demonstrating signs of distress and disorientation.

"What?" He said. The word came to life as a whisper.

"It's okay. Take a minute I'm here. You're here. Everything is going to be okay."

"Sketch." Michael coming around experienced yet again his weighty history crash all at once into his mind, through to the point where Clare told him about the letter and the possibility that there was another member of the Core living in the human world under his nose. Then he knew all the pain to come as he realised, he couldn't give up his search for his fellow energies in the human world. That he couldn't move away from London and their life in the city even if it were to save their relationship.

THIRTY-THREE

The Core

DESPITE HAVING A PLAN, Sketch shook as she approached the vicinity of the One. What she was about to do held enormous risk of failure and would take an Oscar-winning performance to pull off. The One's section of the Core had undergone a makeover that any self-respecting decorating reality show would have been proud to screen to the masses. The space was patterned with rotating spirals of light and dark vibrations which breathed life into the area. In the middle of the spirals was a partially dimmed area with bright circular sections to designate where the One would station himself, like the throne of a King, awaiting his subjects to kneel before him. This is how Sketch found the leader of the Core.

The One sparked and beckoned Sketch to approach. She did so with the required deference and decorum fitting his position in the hierarchy, trusting it would be convincing.

- What brings you to my presence, Sketch?

- I have information.

- We have ascertained there is nothing you can tell me about the humans I don't already know.

- I haven't come to talk about humans. I have become

concerned about the rogue energies. Those who call themselves the Resistance.

- Now that is of interest. Of what nature is this you wish to disclose?

- I can confirm their membership and plans to overthrow your esteemed rule.

- And how is it you have come about this knowledge? Are you one of them?

The light spirals darkened creating an oppressive ambience which added to the weight of Sketch's fear. She pulsed her prepared answer.

- Negative. However, they tried to recruit me. It was during the time I was undergoing the re-education program with Virder. He began to discourse about a different way, about the perils of the regime of the Core, about how he was going to try to usurp you. So, I thought it best to pretend that I was on his side, and so they would let me into the Resistance. I'm not one of them, but they think I am.

- You took it upon yourself to become a double agent?

- I thought it right. Was not that the best thing to do?

- That remains to be seen. I must consider the consequences of your actions. But there may be some value in what you say. I have detained a number of these rebels from the so-called Resistance but require additional evidence before I send them to be recycled. I will need the names of the insurgents to validate your claims.

Sketch realised that this was the point of no return. She might condemn her friends to be sent to an unknown existence outside of the Core. Conflict raged throughout her being, but despite feeling contrary to all her beliefs, she knew that giving up their names was the only chance they had to escape.

- With pleasure.

With reluctance, Sketch proceeded to share the names she knew to be members of the Resistance. Having already outed Virder, next on her list was Pix. She didn't know all the names and thought for a moment about making the rest up but remembered in time that the One would know the identities of all the energies in the Core.

- There are others. Although I've met them, I am not aware of what they have named themselves.

- Would you be able to identify them by their auras? Recognise their signatures?

Sketch hesitated. She hadn't been expecting this. The idea of some kind of identity parade filled her with alarm. There was no going back, no turning around. If she lied now the One would realise.

- Ummm, I think so maybe some of them.

The One's aura sent off sparks of light summoning a couple of nearby energies to his side.

- Bring me the rebels, he demanded.

Sketch noted that his aura had elevated to dark and twisty light. What would her friends think when she stood before them and betrayed them? This was by far the most awful thing she'd ever had to do.

In seconds, before having time to give the matter any further consideration, the One's favoured energies returned with a line of members of the Resistance. Their auras were depleted, but a sense of defiance surrounded them as if they didn't know what might happen to them. Instead, the crucial thing remaining was the hope, however tiny, that they had a chance to transform the Core into the world it used to be. Sketch shrunk before them recognising their dislike of her being. More than anything she wanted to somehow signal the truth to them. But it would be too risky, so instead, she absorbed their hatred and attempted to turn it back on them to convince the One she was on his side.

- Sketch, which of these energies are part of the rebellion?

Sketch paused, looking from one to the other until each of them had been observed.

- All of them.

- Thank you. Your assistance has been invaluable. The One turned to his loyal energies. "Send them for recycling immediately."

"No! Wait. I have an idea." Sketch squirmed, knowing this was the part of her plan where everything might collapse around her.

"What gives you the authority to question my judgement?" asked the One.

"Oh, I don't doubt they should be recycled," said Sketch "But these aren't the only agitators. There are more members of the Resistance. I'm not sure who they are, so if you recycle this lot, we might never find out." She fidgeted, oscillating back-and-forth while waiting for the One to respond.

"That is tempting. However, I'm sure given the nature of punishments about to be brought down upon these miscreants, the rebels will go underground. They'll understand there is no point. That their plots must be abandoned in favour of serving the ultimate authority of the Core - me."

"I haven't thought of that," said Sketch. "They seem very determined. I got no impression they would cease. However, you know better than me. I'm sure you've faced such things before."

Had she just condemned her friends and the Core to a terrible fate?

THIRTY-FOUR

London 2013

ON COMPLETING her final diary entry, Maud tied the numerous notebooks she'd scribbled on for decades up in some purple ribbon purchased years before for this purpose. The colour had faded but still reminded Maud of her old winter coat which she adored. She'd chosen purple as her signature colour because it represented the regal if not royal life she had hoped to achieve. Whether she'd managed to do this was still a question mark in her mind, but she knew she was leaving behind a happy family in Australia and had been the catalyst Sketch needed to remain as a human in this external world. She also hoped she had succeeded in making a lot of people smile.

She placed the spiral bound diaries in a cardboard box and sealed it with sticky-tape. On the top, she placed a note saying the box wasn't to be opened until five years after her death. Time needed to pass for people to grieve. After which they might be ready to dip into her thoughts and musings on life, love and the strangeness of human existence. Five years should be enough for the pain of loss to ease.

She took care to ensure the cat food was topped up, with portions from an automated gizmo she'd bought from Argos, programmed for release at intervals over the next few days. The last thing she wanted was for Clock to be more affected by her departure than necessary. The old feline purred and snaked her way around the old woman's legs as if begging for her to stay by enticing her with soft furry caresses.

"Oh Clock. I'll miss you, but you will have a new home. Everyone loves a cat, and my friends will make sure you are looked after. Thank you for all the love you've given me in your lifetime. I'm not so sure about the half-dead mice you brought me, but your intentions were good. Stay beautiful, lovely being."

With one last look, Maud surveyed her home, blew the building a kiss and exited the house, trailing her shopping trolley behind her.

It was mid-morning when she approached the bustle of Kentish Town Road with its traffic, traders and pedestrians. Her insides began to churn, and she pushed down the vomit which threatened to erupt from her stomach. This couldn't be the end. Surely not. Until now Maud had been sure she must take this path, but perhaps there was an alternative. Maybe she didn't need to die. Her pace slowed to a shuffle, and she took a deep breath trying to take control of heart rate. Since her arrival in London this was the moment she had been waiting for, but now the moment had arrived everything felt wrong. She was a jigsaw piece which looked like it fitted but actually came from a different puzzle.

In her mind were jumbled thoughts and the faces of her son, grandson and daughter-in-law. They were the most compelling reason to stay and Sketch, well wasn't she also a reason to remain in the world? Maud steeled herself and decided to turn back, go home and have a cuppa and some digestive biscuits. Her being in the world wouldn't change things that much, she told herself. She'd keep out of the way or ask John to pay her airfare for a visit to Australia. He was doing well and could afford the money. That's it. That's what she would do.

"Looks like you've got me for a bit longer, world. Bet you weren't expecting that." She beamed at the sky, at the people walking by and a small white fluffy dog sniffing the pavement. Animals were such gorgeous creatures.

Knowing she was now sticking around Maud remembered she had no milk in the fridge and so walked up the road to the nearest Turkish grocery shop. She picked up a pint-sized plastic carton and decided to treat herself to a packet of digestives, the dark chocolate ones which came out of the cupboard on special occasions. After coming to such a momentous decision, it seemed apt to mark the event somehow, and it wasn't like there was anyone to talk to, at least not yet.

She paid the shopkeeper, gave him a twinkly smile and deposited her twenty-six pence change into the collection tin for a charity supporting prisoners who can read to teach prisoners who can't. *What an important cause*, she thought. After packing her purchases into her shopping trolley, Maud set off home to relax, put her feet up and listen to Radio 4. Now she'd be able to listen to all of this week's Book at Bedtime. Not being able to find out what happened at the end of the story had been irritating her.

As she walked down the street, she failed to spot the small, white fluffy dog escape from its owner. The dog scurried along, cutting in front of Maud and wrapping its lead around the wheels of her shopping trolley.

"Oh doggie, what you up to?" she asked.

The dog didn't answer but tried to pull away from the trolley as it lurched to the side. Maud leaned over to steady the cart and found her feet caught up in the tangled lead. She stumbled, fell with the trolley and tumbled into the road and the path of a red London bus.

As everything and everyone in the surrounding area froze for a moment, a packet of dark chocolate digestives rolled out and came to a stop by the wheel of the bus and a trail of spilt milk ran along the road.

THIRTY-FIVE

The Core

TO SKETCH'S RELIEF, the One, after consideration, decided to detain the energies from the Resistance for one human week. Though not as long as Sketch had hoped for, the stay of execution made it possible to enact her rescue plan.

With her now free rein to travel throughout the different zones of the Core, under the guise of tracking down the remaining rebels, Sketch was able to make her way with secrecy to the human user observation area. As she gravitated towards this zone, she recalled numerous times she had assembled with Inco to watch the human boy Matt. Back then she had had the most enormous crush on the teenager. She never imagined she would live in the same house with him as a human, nor had she envisaged the moment when the two of them shared a kiss, lips touching, tongues twirling, making her body and mind lighter than it had ever been. The kiss had been her first but not her first experience of the confusion physical human actions caused. When the kiss occurred, and Matt pulled away from her claiming it was a mistake, a storm of sadness descended in her mind. A storm of thumping blood, tears and the swirling wind of confusion. But now she recalled the moment as pure joy.

The possibility of seeing any of her human friends again filled her with light, but also a competing sense of nervousness. Being in the Core had distorted Sketch's sense of time. Days, weeks, minutes, hours passed differently in the human world, and she had no accurate idea of how long she'd been gone from their world. They might have moved on, stopped looking at the computer because she'd not communicated with them as she'd promised. Would her friends even want her back?

The observation zone was bereft of other energies. Watching the human users was considered less important than fulfilling the actions of the Core to make the computer function to their satisfaction. Sketch disagreed with this notion. She believed the way to serve humans was to understand them. Without an inkling of their motivations or what made them tick the energies were going through a set of prescribed procedures. More often than not this was sufficient, but humans were unpredictable, and Sketch believed knowing as much as possible about them was best. Each of the people living in the human realm was independent of one another, displaying varying personal characteristics, individual reactions to each situation they experienced depending on their life and events they had lived through. This was what made them beautiful, wonderful beings to Sketch and why she had adored being one of them.

The absence of other energies in the zone played to her advantage. Should she have the opportunity to communicate with her friends no one would witness her actions and therefore there would be no repercussions, but she had yet to ascertain how to get a message to them. The One from her former time in the Core had been skilled in this function, so it must be possible, but Virder and the other members of the Resistance had been unable to shed light upon the details of this particular operation. She should, however, be able to see who was on the other side of the computer.

To Sketch's delight the computer was in operation when she arrived. However, no human user sat in front of the monitor. She heard rumbling sounds coming from the kitchen and recognised the surroundings as Trevor's flat. She imagined him making a cup of tea or coffee and then meticulously cleaning up the worktop. She also thought about the deliciousness of a panad, the North Waleian word for a cup of tea. There was something warming, soothing and delicious about the feel of the hot brown liquid going down your throat. It was no wonder that the human inhabitants of London had a particular fondness for the beverage.

She waited for his return and sparked with delight as she saw her former flatmate saunter from the small attic kitchen to the living room of the flat. Sketch urged him to turn around so she could observe his face, but instead, he plonked himself down on the comfy sofa, picked up the remote control and turned on the television. He flicked through the channels until he came across one of their favourite reality TV shows, the one about drag queens. As frustrating as it was not to have his attention, Sketch attempted to join him in viewing the show, revelling in taking part in some essential human activity.

"Trevor," pulsed Sketch. "Turn around. Why don't you know I'm here?" She realised this was a daft question, but part of her thought her friends should be waiting, that they should know when she appeared.

Sketch stayed observing the television screen and the back of Trevor's head for two episodes of the programme. She'd seen both of them before but found it impossible to drag herself away. A little hope niggled at her, telling her that if she just kept observing from her side of the computer things would work out. As the credits rolled for the end of the second show, she hauled herself away knowing that spending any more time at the observation platform would raise suspicion about her actions with the agents of the One. Instead, she continued to gravitate around the different zones of the Core, making it clear she was reporting back to the One and that any rebellious activity would be fed back to the authorities.

THIRTY-SIX

London 2014

"THIS IS BARKING," said Mae. "Off the planet barking." She placed the sheets of paper down on the table and stared at Jackie. "That bit about how this old lady, Maud was one of them computer energies too. Is it some kind of a cult or something?"

"I wish it were that simple," said Jackie. Taking the letter to her side of the table and beginning to re-read the words in her head. If only they'd had this information earlier, they might have been able to prevent this, might have been able to stop Sketch returning to a world which no longer existed. Many unanswered questions began to make sense to Jackie as she took in the words from another decade, but a mountain of others flew into her mind to replace them. Why hadn't Sketch known who Maud was? Why didn't Maud tell anyone who she was? Did this mean there were others from the Core at large in the world? Would they be able to help?

"This is a lot to take in," said Jackie. "We need to take this to Michael. He might have an idea of what to do."

"Will he? Isn't he another crazy cult member who believes in all of this?" Mae wished she'd never met any of these people. Then she would just be getting on with her hair and beauty course and hanging out with cute boys and cute girls and getting drunk every now and again.

"I know you're still struggling to come to terms with this, but I assure you everything I've told you is true. Come with me. Come to Trevor's, and we'll try and talk to Sketch."

Mae rolled her eyes. "If you really want me to come and talk to some computer, I will, but I'm texting a friend to tell them where I am, in case you lot in this cult are dangerous." She whipped out her phone. "What's the address?"

With the location lodged with another teen, the duo left the Townsend's house and headed out in the direction of Trevor's flat.

The door intercom buzzed in Trevor's attic flat rousing him from a disco nap he was having before heading out for a night with some friends. A night which promised to be larger than his ageing body could cope with. Not expecting anyone to come around, he considered ignoring the buzzer. It might be a political campaigner wanting support or someone planning to convert him to the ways of the Lord. Unexpected callers were famous for bringing unwanted messages or bad news. But the buzzing didn't stop so he stumbled over to the door and picked up the intercom phone receiver.

"Hello?"

"Trevor, it's Jackie. I've got news."

"Come on up." He pressed the button letting them in. Jackie's words jolted him into a state of instant awareness. While he couldn't be one hundred per cent certain, he made an educated guess that her news was about Sketch.

Knowing Jackie would take a few minutes to climb up the winding staircase from the ground floor, Trevor wedged open the door and grabbed a beer from the fridge and prised the cap open with a musical bottle opener which played the ill-fated tune to the "Football's coming home" refrain.

When Jackie reached the top of the stairs, she was, as Trevor expected, out of breath. What he hadn't banked on was that she'd brought along a slightly overweight young woman with blue coloured hair. Jackie's companion wheezed and panted with her hands grasping her thighs. Jackie and Trevor exchanged looks.

"This is Mae," said Jackie by way of explanation. "She's Sketch's friend from college."

Mae raised a hand before returning to near asthmatic rasping.

"Oh yeh," said Trevor. "I remember Sketch talking about you. She thought you were tops. And weren't you the one who sent her that Insta pic of that knob Harry snogging Britney?"

"Yeh," said Mae, beginning to regain the power of speech. "Not heard a bean from her since. Not that it was my fault. Harry was a moron. Why don't you have a lift? It's proper cruel making people walk all the way up here."

Before Trevor had a chance to answer, Jackie took control of the conversation. "The reason we're here is we've got some important information about Sketch's world, about the Core."

Mae snorted.

"Ignore her. She's finding it difficult to come to terms with what I've told her about Sketch."

"You told her about Sketch? I thought we'd made a pact not to tell anyone else. They'll be carting us off to the looney bin before we know it."

"Trevor!" said Jackie.

"Sorry, not politically correct. I get it, but Jackie we did say we'd keep this to ourselves."

"It was the only way she'd let me read the letter from Maud."

"Maud, the old lady with the purple coat? What's she got to do with all this?" Trevor's face stretched in directions which were just within the bounds of human ability.

"She knew my Grandma," said Mae. Trevor swigged on his beer bottle and scratched his thinning hair.

"Maud knew lots of people."

"But it turns out Maud wasn't just Maud," said Jackie. "She was from the Core too. She was the One."

Mae shrugged her shoulders, Jackie nodded, and Trevor steadied himself by holding the back of the sofa.

"Oh, this is beginning to feel like a bad Doctor Who story arc with too many characters and we're all the hapless assistants."

"So, if Maud was here at the same time as Sketch how come

you were able to communicate with her as the One in the Core?" asked Trevor.

"That's too much for me even to contemplate," said Jackie.

The buzzer interrupted their question and answer session. "That'll be Michael," said Jackie. "I called him."

"Of course, you did," said Trevor. "Anyone else?"

"Errr, Matt, Ashling and Clare. Is that okay?"

"I'll put the kettle on," said Mae.

THIRTY-SEVEN

The Core

IT TOOK three further attempts before Sketch was able to communicate with any of the humans. The next time she visited the observation zone she found the flat empty, but the computer remained switched on. She took this to be a positive sign. Trevor at least must still be interested in her life in the Core, or it could just be that he needed to use the computer. Perhaps Trevor's laptop had broken, and he was choosing to use the PC as a backup, but she didn't favour this as an option.

Time was a scarce commodity. Only two human days were left in which she needed to make contact and convince them to take part in her plan. Sketch was aware that the One was becoming fractious and demanding answers about the remaining members of the Resistance. Discovering voices coming from the human world the third time she visited the observation zone pushed Sketch into a state of effervescence.

"Ohhh," she exclaimed. "It's Trevor and Inco and Jackie." It didn't escape her notice that Matt was absent from the group, but her feelings for the boy weren't the current priority. Sketch shifted as close as she could to the front of the viewing screen, reducing the distance between her and the three humans and allowing her the fantasy that they were all in the same space.

She was still in this position several moments later when Jackie appeared touching distance from the screen. Sketch observed as she began typing onto the keyboard, each stroke dictated by Michael. From her observation point Sketch was unable to tell precisely what was being typed, but she ascertained that this was some sort of code. Jackie paused and looked up to the monitor and smiled.

"Hello Sketch," she said.

Sketch's aura soared into light. Jackie was speaking to her. Her human friends hadn't forgotten about her because here they were typing code and talking to her through a monitor.

"Hello, Jackie. Hello Trevor, hello... Inco."

Jackie's fingers recommenced typing, bashing away at the keys. Then after a flurry of code, she stopped. Inco and Trevor gathered round on either side of her, and all three looked at the screen and addressed Sketch.

"Sketch, we are hoping you can hear this. We've had no communication with you since you transferred back to the Core. All of us are concerned something has happened to you," said Michael. "Something doesn't feel right, so we've opened up a channel of communication which only you can intercept. If the comms are working, if you can hear us reply by sending one pulse for yes, two for no."

The thought of what they done so excited Sketch that she nearly forgot to send the pulse but when she did it was distinct and indisputable. A cheer went up on the other side of the screen and Trevor fist-pumped Jackie. The humans shot out a series of questions to Sketch.

"Are you in danger?"

Pulse.

"Can we help?"

Sketch's next pulse of light was fainter. She hoped they would be able to assist but didn't know the best way to explain to them what was going on.

"Are you free to communicate with us?"

Pulse. Pulse.

"Do you want us to bring you back?"

Sketch didn't know how to respond to this question. At that moment, she wanted to be clustered around the computer in Trevor's flat with the three of them, but even if a return were possible, that would mean abandoning the Core to the tyranny of the One. She decided not to pulse and waited for the next question.

"Is anyone left from the previous incarnation of the Core?"

Pulse.

Aware that closed question yes and no answers were only going to take them so far, Sketch scrambled through all the data within her reach searching for a means of widening their communication. When the answer came to her, she approximated a grin using the light of her aura, because the solution stood before her like a gigantic obvious thing. She would Morse to them. The energies had, after all, adopted the secret language of Morsing from the human code of the same name. She began to spew out everything she wanted to convey to them as fast as the code would allow.

For the human side of the monitor, she observed furrow brows and looks of confusion, so slowed down the pace of her signals, but the change in speed appeared to make no difference to their comprehension.

"What are you trying to tell us, hon?" asked Jackie. "All we're getting is lots of those flashes on the screen."

Sketch didn't understand why they couldn't interpret the dots and dashes which she sent towards them. She tried again.

"Sorry, Sketch. We don't know what you're trying to say," said Trevor, his face severe but sporting a half sympathetic smile.

There was an impasse between the two sides of the computer. Sketch frustrated to have come so far but unable to enlist the aid of the human trio, and her friends desperate to help but unable to decipher her communications.

"Wait," said Michael. "I've an idea. Who's got the best camera on their phone?" The three pulled out their mobiles and in a glance selected Trevor's mobile as the smartest tech-wise of the bunch. Michael addressed the screen. "Okay, Sketch. Try starting from the beginning again. I'm going to video you, and then we can work out what you are trying to say."

From the depths of the Core, Sketch wished to hug Michael. Instead, she gave a bright affirmative pulse before sharing with them the critical parts of her story and the fate awaiting the Resistance and her fellow energies. The game was on.

THIRTY-EIGHT

London 2014

IN THE CROWDED space of Trevor's flat, Michael endeavoured to work out how he was going to tell Clare about his change of heart and that he no longer wanted to move away to the north of England to begin their lives anew. His thoughts flipped between this problem and locating ways to communicate with Sketch in the Core. It was clear that something had gone badly wrong for her not to been in touch. Either that or the new world inside the Core was brave, fulfilling and happy. He suspected the former option had a higher probability of being what happened. If this was the case, then he had a duty to do everything possible to bring order back to their former world, because a greater part of him was energy than human.

All the humans huddled around the computer, staring at the screen as if by increasing the number of eyes with sight of it increased the chances of Sketch making contact with them. Michael sighed, struggling with the illogical nature of their thinking.

"Michael, you know the most about this. What can we do to let Sketch know we want to speak to her? Other than talking to the screen that is." Michael sought an answer to Trevor's question.

"There might be a way with coding to send a message, but there are no guarantees that the communication will go directly to Sketch. Anyone in the Core might interpret it."

"And that makes a difference?" asked Matt. "Won't whoever gets the message tell Sketch?"

Michael raised his eyebrows. "That's not how it works."

"How does it work then? said Matt in a voice that suggested to Michael he was irritated.

"In simple terms, the Core operates by rigid hierarchy. The realm is headed up by a super entity called the One. The One has the power to make all decisions relating to energies in the Core. Their function is to ensure human users are supported all time and are able to access the functions of the computer."

Matt's fingers drummed on the desk. Michael glared at him, frustrated by his impatience.

"If the energies are obliged to serve us humans, shouldn't Sketch be replying to us?" asked Matt.

"Communication between computer energies inside the Core and human use is strictly regulated and rare. It is not preferable for humans to have an awareness of existence for you do not have the capacity to comprehend the complex nature of the universe."

Matt stood up and paced around the room; his hands forced into the pockets of his jeans.

"Yep, I know you think we're all a bit thick and inferior, but is there anything you can do?"

"Okay Matt," said Jackie. "Let's all just cool down. Everyone wants Sketch to get in touch, and it's no one's fault we've not heard anything. I think maybe both of you should take a break and get some fresh air or something."

"Yes," said Clare. "Let's go out to get some coffee."

Inside Michael began to boil. He had no control over the situation, and despite feeling the love Clare was trying to show him, his overwhelming desire was to hide alone under the duvet in a darkened room. It was as if he'd travelled back in time to his early days in the human world when he didn't know who he was and the pressures of living that way had forced his mind into a dark solitude.

"Alright, but just for a bit," he said. "Now we know what we do it's important someone is here, in case Sketch sends a signal."

"I'll be here," said Trevor. "I have stuff to do, and I live here."

Clare steered her partner away from the computer desk and the group of people affecting his mood and behaviour. Michael knew he was being unreasonable. He understood the effect this would be having on Clare and told himself to moderate his actions and words to those that would be expected by reasonable humans in such a circumstance. "Sorry," he mumbled to her as they went down the stairs to the outside door. "I'm finding this difficult." Clare didn't say anything, and Michael, unsure as to how best to follow up his short statement stayed quiet too.

They walked for about ten minutes until reaching a quiet-ish cafe in Tufnell Park's main shopping street. Clare took control, ordering them both strong, black coffees, and herded Michael to a table in the back corner opposite the toilets where they could talk undisturbed.

At first, they sat staring at their coffees, playing with spoons while failing to address the elephant in the room. The silence was broken by Clare. "This means we're not moving, doesn't it? Don't answer. I don't need an answer. I already know it. I don't even know why I bothered asking the question."

"I'm sorry," said Michael taking her hand. "If things were different."

"But they're not."

"No."

"I love you. Part of loving you has always been knowing you're not like everyone else. That's what makes you-you. This is all been incredibly hard for me. But I haven't at any point stopped loving you."

"And I love you," said Michael. "I love you as much as any human."

A tear tumbled down his face, and Clare wiped it away. "Which takes us back to the problem. You're not human." Michael began to speak. "No wait," said Clare "Let me finish. You're not human, and you can't live here without knowing what happened to all your fellow energies, so we'll stay in London. I'll continue with the business and support you to find them if that's what you want. But you have to be here for me, you have to love me still and want me, want this, want us."

She looked at him, her eyes were begging him to say yes.

"Yes, I want us, but I might have to go at least in the short term. Someone has to help Sketch, and I think I might be the only one who can do it."

THIRTY-NINE

The Core & London 2014

A SUITABLE AMOUNT of time went by before Sketch revisited the human user observation zone, giving Trevor, Michael and Jackie enough time to work out what Sketch's random pulses meant. She calculated this based on their combined intellect and Michael had the advantage of his alter ego Inco's time as a computer energy to draw on. Before propelling her being to the area, Sketch made sure she was not being followed by the One's fervent supporters. She eased her way in front of the viewing panel and lit up with excitement to see not only Jackie, Michael and Trevor sitting around the monitor but also Matt, Ashling, Dominic and Sammy. She pulsed using Morse to test if they had cracked the code.

"Look how much Sammy has grown!"

The group paused and stared up at Michael as he plugged the information into his phone and repeated her words to the group.

"Sketch!" cried Ashling. "It's really you. They told me, but I couldn't believe it. And yes, Sammy has outgrown his clothes twice since you saw him last." Everyone waved at the screen, said their hellos and grinned until Michael hushed them.

"The Morse Code was clever, Sketch," he said. "But what is

happening in the Core is horrifying. We must take action, and I think I know what we should do."

It was wonderful to have someone to share the pressure of the situation with and not to feel everything rested up the decisions which she considered to be uninformed. She recognised Michael, not just as the man who was married to her college tutor Clare, but as Inco the energy who was her best friend during her time training. It mattered not a jot that he was in an older body or that his form was human. The important factor was the level of understanding he brought to the situation.

"Oh, tell me Inco? We are required to act with haste as there are fewer human hours left than we need."

"After discussion here, we all think it would be helpful for you to have another energy on your side. So..."

"So, he's going to jump back into the computer with you," said Matt, his face screwed up like a child who's been told to share his toys. Jackie glared at her son.

"What? You can't do that. What about Clare?" said Sketch.

"We've spoken about this, and she understands. This is a temporary measure. To put right the things which are unbalanced, out of kilter, unhinged."

Sketch wondered if Clare was as understanding as Inco made out. She imagined she would not be so happy if something similar happened to her.

"But how will you get here? Transform back to an energy I mean?"

"That's one part we do know how to do," said Jackie. "Do you remember the device we used to attempt to send you back to the Core the first time?"

Sketch morsed a yes.

"Well, I still have the device, and it turns out the thing is still functional. Michael here has checked it out and we're ninety per cent certain everything will go to plan."

The computer energy looked to each one of the group gathered in Trevor's flat. None of their faces or body language gave her confidence that they were even fifty per cent certain. "Are you sure?"

"Yes," said Michael. "I am aware of backdoors through the Core and can lead us to where the Resistance is being held. As a group, we can capture the One, reveal the truth and return the Core to its former glory."

"And be home in time for tea," added Trevor, who couldn't resist blowing Sketch a kiss.

"And you're sure Clare is okay with this? Where is she?" asked Sketch.

"She's taking a class at the moment, but she knows this might happened," said Michael.

Sketch turned her attention to Matt, his scowl still stuck to his face. She didn't have the words to make things better for him, so instead morsed a generic message of love to the group.

"I'll see you all very soon," she said. "I'm sure of it. Michael, are you ready to do this?"

He nodded and handed his phone with the Morse decoder app to Matt. Sketch couldn't help but giggle a little as Sammy tried to grab at the phone thinking he could play a game.

Jackie gestured to the others to move away to the corners of the room. They called their 'goodbyes' and 'love yous' to Sketch as Michael stationed himself close to the computer and Jackie inserted a USB stick in the shape of a Lego brick into the slot at the front of the machine. Then she too stepped back.

"The code is now on the smartphone ready to be transmitted," he said to Sketch. "Matt will activate the device and I will be with you in the Core in a matter of seconds."

Sketch pulsed encouragement in Michael's direction steadied herself for a disturbance in the space around her and stared in Matt's direction, remembering the sensation of touching lips with him. She shivered as he pressed down on the phone's screen and Michael's body became pixellated and disappeared from Trevor's living room. She observed a collective holding of breath as they waited for Sketch to confirm his arrival in her world.

On her side of the computer, she danced, spun and sparked bright lights like silent monochrome fireworks as Michael teleported into the observation area of the Core beside her and became Inco once again.

FORTY

The Core

BEING in the same space as Inco after so many human months had gone by uplifted Sketch's spirit to a level, she'd forgotten she could reach.

"Inco."

"Sketch."

In that distinct moment they were transported out of the danger and stress and to a place where they were just them. Sketch struggled to equate the beings they were in pure energy form to the physical human avatars both had inhabited outside of the computer.

"We are here," said Sketch with a surge of wonder.

The spell cloaking them from reality dissipated in moments. Truth was much more powerful than the magic their reunion could conjure up, and despite her desire to ask a million questions about Inco's life since she'd last seen him, Sketch pushed on with dealing with the immediate crisis.

"How are we going to rescue them? The One's domain is guarded at all times, and his energies demonstrate the utmost loyalty. I don't know how we will be able to get past them."

"In that direction is a little-known pathway through the light passages of the Core. Think of it like an Easter Egg hidden in a

DVD or a computer game, but this is disguised, so the route is next to impossible to locate unless you have been told its position."

"Really? I wasn't aware such things were utilised in the Core. That's very exciting." She loved the idea of being privileged to such secret information. Inco must have been held in high esteem during his time as a cursor to enable him access to this kind of knowledge. There was much she didn't know about him and not just about his life as Michael.

"Can you call on the remaining members of the Resistance to set up a distraction for us?"

Sketch pulsed in the affirmative. "Yes, I will leave an energy trace at the meeting point. This instructs the Resistance to enact the distraction plan. But the message will take a short time before being received by the Resistance energies."

"Then we'll have some time to catch up. You can't imagine how it feels to see you again after all these years."

His pulses struck Sketch and made her wobble. She had been in the human realm for less than a year, but Inco had spent a lifetime there. To a teenage human, he was ancient. And then there was Clare.

"I've missed you too. Being alone or thinking you are the only one of your kind is horrible."

Their auras touched briefly before she gravitated away towards the assigned meeting point. Virder, thinking ahead had set up the rendezvous place in advance for emergencies, and this seemed to fit the definition of an emergency. The few energies who escaped being rounded up by the agents of the One ensured Sketch knew where it was and the protocol for activating the communications chain. They had also agreed on the distraction plan in advance. The blue screen of death meltdown could only be used sparingly without attracting attention. That would defeat the object. So instead they opted for a screen freeze. In such a circumstance the computer couldn't be reactivated without the input of a user, a human user who would be required to hit escape alt and delete at the same time and attempt to shut down the inactive programmes. Sketch hoped that no one in Trevor's flat would try to do this with any haste, but even if they did or went further and rebooted the machine, the Resistance had boobytrapped the processes so the mechanical beast would take longer than usual to get back to being a functional computer. The energies would all be summoned to their stations to minimise the disruption caused to the users.

A swirl of energy in the shape of the infinity symbol marked the space where Sketch left her trail. On the way back to meet with Inco, she paid extra heed to appear to scrutinise the energies around her wanting them to be aware she was an agent of the One. Their auras dimmed as she moved into their spaces and she sensed a shift when she glides away.

"All done," she pulsed to Inco.

"As a precaution, I think we should exchange thoughts in the language you call Morse," he replied. "It will also be of a faster pace now we can both sense each other's auras."

"That's an excellent idea. Did you always have such strategic thoughts, or did you pick them up in your human body?"

"Sketch."

"Inco."

"My experience was divergent from yours. When I transformed, I lost my data download and any sense of who I was. I awoke with a body, no clothes, no identity in the middle of someone else's house. And I was decades from where I had been sent."

"Woah! I can't imagine what that must have been for you. My transformation went to plan, and it still took forever before I got used to having a body and all the swirly emotions and hormones. But being human was good wasn't it?" She began to fizz at the memories of her bodily existence.

"In the end," said Inco. "My youth was troubled."

"Did you get drunk and have an awful hangover?"

Inco didn't reply prompting a growing level of awkwardness in Sketch like she was a silly gawky teen who spouted drivel and caused embarrassment.

"Sorry, I didn't mean to be flippant just that I thought...oh I don't know what I thought."

"All of that happened to me and more. Mostly I spent my life trying to find out who I was and for a big part of it who you were. The first word I spoke, over and over again was Sketch."

"If I'd known."

"If you'd known what? There was nothing you could have done. We were out of sync, out of space, out of time."

"But life was ok in the end. And you and Clare, you look pretty happy. You have someone to be with."

"Yes, my life with Clare saved me."

"Saved by human love," mused Sketch, her morses blocked for his senses by the frozen screen alarm signalling all energies to follow the emergency protocols.

FORTY-ONE

The Core

THE BACK ROUTE to the area inhabited by the One proved as undetectable as Inco had claimed. Sketch scuttled behind him, attempting to be both inconspicuous and elegant. How he weaved through the vast zones of the Core unseen by the energies on alert inspired her. They moved between light fluctuations and Inco manipulating them to open new channels they slid through out of sight and unnoticed. What amazed Sketch was how easy it appeared for Inco to reintegrate back into the Core and live without a phys-ical case - the skin, muscle and bone of the homo sapiens body. He gave the appearance through his unwavering aura and memory of how to navigate through the secret passageways of the Core that he'd been back for a considerable time or had never left at all. For Sketch the return had been much harder than that although she guessed he had a mission, had come back for a purpose knowing what the situation was.

Inco spinned another spectrum of light and opened up the final pathway.

"When we go through, we will still be hidden. I will survey the area to see if we are safe to proceed."

"And if it's not?" asked Sketch.

"I haven't thought that far ahead."

Both energies steadied their auras and emerged through the pathway into the arena of the One. The spiralling columns of light were familiar to Sketch, but they took on a new level of interest as she observed Inco move from one to another using them to disguise his presence. *Ah, that's how he does it,* she thought. He was gone only a short time before returning to her side.

"Did you see what I did? How I moved?"

Sketch affirmed that this was the case.

"It is safe for us to proceed only if you do exactly as I did, follow me and we will reach the area in which the rebels are being held captive." He waited until he was sure Sketch had understood his morses and then gestured for them to proceed.

Sketch stayed close to his presence, vibrating like a bundle of nervousness. They moved with the flow, curving their way from pillar to pillar until Inco came to a sudden halt. Sketch nearly bashed into him, but steadied herself before they could collide.

He employed low tone vibrations, morsing to Sketch to stay still and not to attract attention. She became aware why when the One and his entourage swept past the pillar of light which protected them from sight. She contained herself thinking they had no backup plan or any idea what they would say when confronted by their evil leader. Her thoughts became dark and spirally until she glanced towards Inco and noticed his calm presence. If he could remain unfazed, then she could too. A short period elapsed after which Inco indicated for them to continue their journey. The One had moved far from sight, far from the place where he could detect their auras with ease. Sketch released a warming glow, the equivalent of a human sigh of relief and following this change in her aura Inco led her through a light filter behind which she could detect vibrations and a dim glow of aura which belonged to Virder, Pix and the other captive members of the Resistance. They both checked around to make sure it was safe before she let out a massive explosion of light expressing her joy to see her friends again.

"Yeah young un," said Virder. "What took you so long?"

"Well, getting here was a smidgen complicated," said Sketch.

"First of all, I had to find everyone who remained in the Resistance. Then I had to lie so horribly, oh, you may have heard about my lies, the things I had to say about you to the One. I didn't mean any of it." Sketch watched everyone to gauge their reaction. So worried was she that they wouldn't understand why she acted in the way she did that she felt an urge to flee.

"Oh Sketch," said Pix lightning with each word. "I always knew you wouldn't betray us. Such a characteristic is not in your nature. We saw how you behaved in the human world, and you could be trusted."

"Really? You are watching me all the time?"

"Why yes."

"We were indeed," added Virder. "Ever since you were a trainee, I've been paying attention to you. Always knew you had the potential for greatness. Though I don't think you had any clue." The senior energy turned his focus towards Inco. "Good to see you again. I'm guessing you are here to rescue us."

"Yes, we have to move quickly. Do you have the activation codes?"

"The activation codes?" asked Sketch "What are they for?" Inco and Virder moved as close to each other as was possible.

"To set things right, we are required to take drastic action. This means we need to reformat the hard drive of the Core."

Sketch found herself spinning around and around as she attempted to process the implications of what Virder had morsed. Had she misinterpreted the signals or their meaning? If not, his words meant all the energies in the current iteration of the Core would be sent to another realm, transformed into different energy forms unable to return to the computer. It represented a total reset, back to factory settings, leaving the Core a blank space for new energies to inhabit it.

"Is there a plan? is there a transformation plan?" asked Sketch.

Pix moved towards Sketch, expressing a soft light that cloaked Sketch's aura. "It's not safe. The plan, it's not safe."

"Why?"

"Because the plan is the One's plan," said Inco in low tone

vibrations. "This is far from ideal, but we do have the power to dictate where some of the energies will go."

"How many can we save?" asked Sketch.

"Three," said Virder. "Only three. Two can be sent to the human world and another to the animal realm. The rest. Well, the rest will be randomly transformed and dispersed."

FORTY-TWO

The Core

THE IDEA of being randomly transformed into an energy of any kind was abhorrent to any sentient energy. These were the ones who were aware of the real nature of the universe and how it operated. Many lifeforms, pebbles, humans, waves, pigeons, and macadamia nuts had no idea about transformation. Computer energies did.

Sketch looked for Pix to Virder to Inco, and the other energies stood around them. "That's terrible," she said. "How can we make that decision? The humans would call this playing God."

"We have to apply logic to the situation," said Virder. She could see he was being serious, but she didn't still understand the ease at which he felt that they might make such a decision. "I don't have that kind of logic anymore," she said. "The months I spent with humans have given me a wider perspective. Not everything has a logical answer. These are lives we are dealing with, making decisions about." Virder sighed. "I comprehend you have experience of things we cannot understand; however, this is the only way." There was a resignation coupled with certainty in his words. Sketch was aware of the dilemma he must be facing for it was the same one in front of them all.

"I'm not comfortable with this. I'm not. But if as you say there are no other options then okay. But how do we decide who to transform?"

Pix began to pulse. "The easiest way with the greatest chance of success is to send to energies who have already been in human form back to their world. And to be clear by that, I mean you Inco and you Sketch."

"No!" said both Inco and Sketch. The other energies stared at them, a wall of resolute determination and displayed no sign of changing their perspective on the matter. "Well, I won't go," said Sketch. "There are so many energies who are worthier than me. Let one of them take my place. What about Pix? She can do wonderful things in the world."

Virder took his turn to speak. "Pix has already been allocated to transform to the animal realm."

"I'm to be a cat, Sketch. An important cat."

"Oh, I've always thought being a cat would be most pleasant," said Sketch. "Being looked after in bed sleeping whenever you want to, going out roaming around in the world, exploring, meeting other cats and then coming home curling up on the bed or a windowsill. You will love being a cat Pix."

"That's a wonderful thing to hear," said her friend. "Did you ever have a cat?"

Sketch still distracted by the lovely idea of her friend becoming an animal began to grow and sparkle little as she remembered the furry bundle of feline fun she'd inherited from Maud when she died.

"Yes, I had a cat called Clock. And what a magnificent creature she was."

"Clock." Pix morsed the word as if exploring its viability. "That's unusual. I approve."

Virder vibrated interrupting all the chat about kitties.

"Little time remains. We have no option left nor have we the capacity to debate the situation further. Sketch, you have to return to the human world along with Inco and ensure the hard drive is reset from the human side. This will only work if it is enacted in both the Core and the exterior of the computer. However, once this action is complete one of you is required to return here to greet the new energies, train them, teach them the right way and become the One."

Before either of them could respond to the sounds of the signal created by the distraction alert, it began to slow indicating that the Core was about return to normal.

"We must act now. I have the codes required. Inco, do you have yours?"

"Yes. I am ready; the plan is logical."

Things moved so quickly that Sketch had a trivial amount of time to comprehend what was about to occur. All the energies populating the Core aside from herself, Inco and Pix would be transformed.

"But Virder. You could end up anywhere."

"That is my fate, young Sketch. I have been a computer energy for more than my allotted time. I will go where the universe sends me and play my part." Although they were on different sides of an invisible barrier Sketch and Virder faced one another, sharing sparks with one another in a mutual understanding that this is how it had to be.

Virder commenced the process. He pushed out a series of codes using the traditional binary language preferred by computer energies. The distraction alert stopped, and the area was flooded with light and an influx of hostile energies. Virder sped up his recitation of the codes and handed over to Inco to complete the process. The energies loyal to the One encroached into the space, backing the rebels into a corner. Sketch, Pix and Inco found themselves protected by an energy shield while Inco rambled through the remaining codes and gestured Pix and Sketch to gather round and combine their auras. With no human seconds to spare, the sequence was complete. Sketch felt herself pixelate for the second time and disperse away from her home in the Core towards the human world.

"Goodbye, young un," pulsed Virder before the Core began to shut down.

FORTY-THREE

London 2014

DESPITE HAVING UNDERGONE a transformation from the form of an energy to that of a human once before, Sketch threw up as soon as she took on a solid form. She failed to notice her friends around her as the rainbow of colours scattered around Trevor's living room assaulted her visual cortex like an unexpected slap.

"Oh, that hurts," she said sinking to the ground clasping her head.

"Not there!" said Jackie, angling Sketch away from the pile of sick she'd deposited on the carpet. "Sit here, on the sofa." Sketch sunk down closed her eyes and fell asleep.

"How?" asked Mae. "How is it possible? Have you given me drugs? Am I on acid or mushrooms or something?"

"No," said Matt. "What you saw is real. That was Sketch and Michael travelling from the Core of the computer to here, pixel by pixel. Mum told, I told you, everyone told you."

"I know but."

"Yeh, blue-haired girl. It's a lot."

"Can someone give me a hand with Michael?" said Clare who was sat on the floor cradling the head of her returned husband, stroking his hair. "He's not coming around."

Trevor and Ashling darted across the room to help, leaving Mae staring at Sketch and muttering inaudible comments related to her shock and realisation that her friend wasn't at all what she'd seemed. Matt sat down next to Sketch on the other side of the sofa from his mother, cushioning Sketch.

"Matt. Jackie. What? Where?" said Sketch.

"Shush hon, you're still disorientated from the journey. It'll take a little while."

"Yeh, take it easy Sketch. You're safe now. You're back in our world," said Matt. His hand hovered over hers for seconds before he withdrew it.

"Inco, did Inco make it? And what about Pix?"

Matt and Jackie glanced and one another and shrugged.

"Inco's here. He's with Clare. Who is Pix, Sketch? Only two of you who came through."

"She's my friend. She's brave and funny and oh. She's an animal. Are there any animals?" Sketch attempted to get up from her seated position but was overcome by a spell of dizziness.

"You really must sit for a bit hon. I'm sorry about your friend, but we've not seen anyone but Michael and yourself. Rest a little, and then we can talk. When your brain is at full capacity, it will be easier to think about where she might be."

On the far side of the room, Clare and Trevor had placed Michael into the recovery position and covered him with a blanket from the sofa.

"Why isn't he waking up?" asked Clare.

"It must put a real stress on you, being all non-physical, without a body and then landing here with the gravity and the colours and the noise. Sketch told me about her first time."

"Yeh, give him a bit of time," said Ashling squeezing Clare's shoulder in solidarity.

"Seeing him appear like that. I mean, I believed him but watching it happen makes it seem hyper-real," said Clare. "Michael, please talk to me."

"Shall I get him some water?" asked Ashling.

"Thanks, that would be great. Could you get some for me too?"

said Clare. Ashling backed off and beckoned Trevor to join her. They huddled together in the kitchen and whispered their conversation.

"What should we do?" asked Ashling.

"I dunno. He's not looking very good. I'm half wondering if we should call an ambulance."

"The NHS is fab, but I'm not sure they'll have a clue what to do for what appears to be a sort of teleport sickness."

"At least they'll be able to monitor his physical symptoms. Did you know when he first came through, he didn't speak for months?"

"No, how d'you know that?"

"Clare told me," said Trevor still whispering. "She's been around a lot lately. Not at the same time as Michael. I think she just wanted someone to talk to about it. She spent a lot of time just staring at the computer like Sketch was about to leap out of it."

"Wow," said Ashling. "Look, I think we should give it a couple of hours and see how he does. He's not had a dangerous fall so we could move him to your bed. It'd be comfier than the floor."

"Ok, let's suggest that to Clare and see what she says."

Trevor and Ashling shared the first stages of their plan with Clare, holding the back the idea about calling the paramedics, not wanting to scare her more than was necessary.

"Between the four of us, we should be able to move him without causing him any damage or discomfort. Matt, can you give us a hand?" asked Trevor.

Matt turned from his space on the sofa next to Sketch. "Hang on. Sketch, I'll be right back." She moved her head up and down slowly.

Matt and Trevor raised Michael from the floor, supporting him with his arms wrapped around their shouldered they resembled a couple of human crutches. Clare held his head to prevent it from lolling around as Ashling went ahead to open the door and make sure there the bed was tidy. They placed him in the middle, restored the recovery position, left him lying next to his wife and tiptoed out of the room.

"Matt," said Jackie. "I need you to go back to ours and pick up something."

"Sure, what do you need?"

"This is going to sound a little odd but bring Clock, her food and her litter tray. Sketch keeps asking for her."

"That does sound weird. I've got to go back anyway. Dominic's going out, so I need to pick up Sammy."

"Oh, the combination of Sammy and Clock is perfect. Bring them both over as soon as you can. There's some food for the little one in the fridge. It needs heating up in the microwave. Let's hope it's not got any rogue energies inside of it."

FORTY-FOUR

London 2014

WHEN JACKIE DEEMED Sketch to be well enough, she made her a cup of tea and fed her a packet of bourbon biscuits she found amongst the snacks piled up in one of the cupboard shelves in Trevor's kitchen.

"Biscuits are good," said Sketch whose cheeks were now showing some colour compared with their former pallid state. "Where is Inco? I mean Michael?"

"He's lying down in Trevor's room. His transition wasn't as smooth as yours," said Jackie, taking Sketch's hand in hers.

"But he's okay?"

"To be honest, I'm not sure. This isn't something we know very much about, in fact, we don't know anything."

"Can I see him?"

"In a bit," said Jackie. "There's something I need to show you first." Jackie pulled her bag on her lap and looked inside. It didn't take her long to find what she was looking for. In her hand was an envelope, the envelope containing Maud's letter to Sketch. "I could try and tell you what this says, what it is, and what it means, but I think its best if you read for yourself," said Jackie. She passed the letter to Sketch. Sketch opened the envelope and read from the beginning.

Dear Sketch,

'By the time you get this letter we will have met in the human world, but I will be gone. You knew me as two different entities. As Maud the older lady living in North London in the human world. Your friend who dies. But you also knew me as the One. The entity who sent you from the Core to a distant realm where you knew no one.

Before it was my time to leave, I watched over you hoping to guide you, and as you read this, I'm sure you'll be wondering why I didn't tell you who I really was and how to get back to the Core. But I couldn't. I couldn't change matters as they were supposed to play out. Some things are fixed and cannot be changed. It's not always clear which they are, but your stay, your life and your activities in the human world were mandated. Another of those events which could not be altered; which cannot be altered, is my death. Do not mourn me more than any human for this is my gift to the world.

I write this now as a younger woman than you know me and I hope no unforeseen event prevents this letter reaching you at the appropriate time because this letter is a warning and an explanation. Why am I in the human world? Well, after you left the Core, a hostile takeover took place, and I was forced to activate the emergency protocols and disperse all of the energies into different realms. Not everything went to plan. While I arrived exactly where I'm supposed to be a number of the energies ended up in the wrong form or in the wrong decade or in the wrong town, sometimes a combination of these. I don't know where they all are and at the moment, I am alone in your world for this is your world now, the human world.

Don't go back. Don't attempt to return to the Core because we're not there and only a dangerous rogue energy is in situ. The rest of us have left.

Live your life Sketch. Live it with a joie de vivre, travel, see the beautiful places of the planet. Find people to love and settle with and keep the spirit of the Core alive amongst those around you.

I am privileged to have met you as a human. I waited for many years. I know this because I saw my life from inside the Core. I knew everything that awaited me when I transformed. You learned to be one of the best humans I have met in my time here. Be kind, be beautiful inside and out and smile, smile whenever you can.

All my love, Maud.'

The letter fell from Sketch's fingers onto the floor. She looked up at Jackie with her eyes filled with tears and said a single word full of emotion.

"Maud."

Instead of replying with words Jackie took Sketch in her arms and gave her the biggest cuddle she could bestow. She took a tissue from her pocket and wiped the tears from under Sketch's eyes.

After a few minutes, she sat up. "Better?"

"A little," said Sketch. "I understand more now, but I wish I'd known who she was."

"Then you would've thought of things differently. You had to discover things this way."

Sketch sniffed. "That makes logical sense, but it doesn't stop me feeling sad and missing Maud even more."

"Can you tell us what happened inside the Core?" Said Jackie.

"Of course, but first I need to see Inco. There might be something I can do to help."

"Let me go and check first with Clare. It's really up to her," said Jackie.

Left alone on the sofa, Sketch surveyed her familiar surroundings. Torn between being content at being back and safe, she also was filled with a sense of profound sadness that all those energies were needlessly transformed and lost across time and space. The One, Maud, had selflessly given up two lives, two existences to save both Sketch and the Core. How could Sketch now stay in the human world knowing the consequences of inappropriate leadership inside the computer?

Her thoughts were interrupted by the buzz of the doorbell. Being nearer than anyone else in the flat, Sketch got up to answer see who was there.

"Hello."

"Sketch," came a voice which made her body sing. "It's me, Matt."

"Come in." She buzzed him in and waited by the door, not sure how to greet him given the way that they parted when she last was in the human world. But her dilemma didn't last long as she discovered he was accompanied by both Sammy and Clock the cat. Sammy jumped at her and grabbed her legs.

"Sketch, where have you been?" he squealed.

"On an adventure Sammy. One day I'll tell you all about it. Why don't you run through to the kitchen and ask mummy for a biscuit? Tell her Trevor keeps the best ones in the plastic box at the back of the cupboard."

She ruffled his hair and turned to Matt.

"Hello."

"Hello."

"Come here stupid," she pulled him in for a hug, forcing him to stick his arm carrying the cat carrier to the side. "I've missed you."

"Me too, and I'm sorry, you know for, well I'm just sorry," said Matt. "Got to put the cat down." He pulled away from her arms but replaced her hug with an enormous grin.

"Me too," said Sketch. She bent down and opened the cat basket releasing Clock from her confines. "Hello little Clock, or should I call you Pix?" She buried her face in the fur of the kitty and heard the cat purr in reply. If only she could speak feline but that wasn't a skill given to her from her original data download.

"It's so good to know you're here. I'm going to need someone to help me bring Inco back into his human form."

Clock meowed and rubbed her furry face against Sketch's skin.

FORTY-FIVE

London 2014

THOUGH SADDENED by the contents of Maud's letter, Sketch was bolstered by the appearance of Clock, a cat who turned out to be of greater significance than she could have imagined when she agreed to take her in. Had Maud known that Clock was, in fact, an energy from the new iteration of the Core? Given the age of the cat and her adoption by Maud, it was impossible to know. Sketch wasn't sure how much had been predetermined for Maud, but she got a sense as an energy that she had sufficient free will to influence what might happen next, both for the humans and the future of the Core. For both, she wished benevolence with a giant heap of fun thrown in because life, no matter what form it took, could be hard and a smile and injection of the stuff that makes children laugh always went some way to make it better.

After a tap on the door to Trevor's bedroom, Sketch edged her way through the gap, conscious not to disturb any moments between Clare and Michael. Clare lay next to her husband, her arms cradling him as if he was about to fall off a ledge.

"Is it okay to come in?" asked Sketch, her voice just above a whisper.

"Sure."

"Any change?"

Clare shook her head. "It's as if his body is here, but his mind is trapped somewhere else. Is that even possible?"

Sketch sat on the bed next to them as Clare readjusted her body to an upright position, her hand still holding onto Michael's arm.

"I'm not sure. Transformation is supposed to a complete thing, but there was a reset going on and that, it turns out, can be unpredictable and a bit messy."

"I just want him back. The Michael I've loved all these years, but it's never going to be the same even if he wakes up."

"He'll wake up," said Sketch hoping her words would be in some way reassuring but suspecting that wouldn't be the case. "And he's still Michael."

"You think? He changed when he remembered who he really was. And then there's you." Clare's tone changed making Sketch feel uncomfortable with the direction the conversation was going. "Where do you fit into this horrible four-dimensional jigsaw?"

Sketch didn't answer the question. She didn't have a response. Not because she couldn't find the words but because she had no answer herself. Michael as Inco was her closest friend. She loved him, but she'd seen a different side to him when he came to their rescue in the Core. There was much she didn't know about him. And then there was Matt. Matt, the human boy who she had kissed. The thought of kissing was bittersweet. What use is a beautiful kiss if it fills you with indescribable uncertainty?

Clare looked away. "Is there anything you do know? Anything that might help to wake him up?"

"I'm sorry. I really wish there was."

Tears welled up in Clare's eyes. "No, I'm sorry. This isn't your fault. You're as much a victim here as the rest of us."

"I can't think that way. The victim bit I mean. There has to be a way through this."

Clare sniffed and wiped her eyes on the back of her hand. "Do you think you could keep an eye on him while I go to the loo and freshen up a bit?"

"Of course. And get some food too. Food always helps. In fact, tell Trevor we need a round of sausage sarnies."

Clare managed a small smile as she gathered herself up, leaving Sketch alone with Michael for the first time since their return.

Sketch looked at him. He was so old as a human and while she knew with all the logic afforded to her as a computer energy that this was just a physical casing and not the person itself, she couldn't help but see him through her human eyes.

"Hey, Inco. It's strange calling you that here. But maybe you can hear me, and if you can, then I will attempt to help you in the way you assisted us in the rescue of the Core. Not that I'm sure rescue is the right word." She paused, half expecting him to open his eyes and answer her, but nothing happened. She took his hand in hers, conscious of doing so and it felt alien.

"Why is this happening to us?"

She sat attempting not to cry for a life now gone. Her hand experienced the sensation of being squeezed not once but again and again.

"Oh! You're morsing. You can hear me. Say what you said again." She listened with her hand as Michael squeezed short and long pulses to her.

"You are both here and in the Core? How is that possible?"

He replied, and her translation into English sped up as the ability to morse returned to her.

"I don't know either. Did the reset work?" She began to reply in the same language, synchronising her communications with his.

"It concluded successfully, but someone needed to be here to welcome the newcomers," said Inco.

"But I thought we could decide that afterwards. From here. From the human world."

"Virder was ill-informed about the process. I always knew this required me to be present."

"But your body, why is it in Trevor's flat?"

"That I don't know."

"It is distressing Clare."

There was a silence between their hands before Inco recommenced the conversation. "You must look after her. Explain that this is the only way. It is the optimum solution for us all."

"But she loves you. You love her. Don't you?"

"Yes, but Sketch, what you haven't learnt yet, is love is never enough. Not on its own."

"I don't believe you." Tears rolled down her cheeks onto their hands, coating them with the salty water computer energies were unable to produce.

"That might be so, but it is the truth. Goodbye, Sketch. Live a happy and productive life."

FORTY-SIX

London 2014

THE FLAT WAS CRAMPED with everyone gathered around eating whatever snacks could be liberated from Trevor's kitchen cupboards. A plan to get takeaway was vetoed after no one could decide on what type of cuisine they wanted, leaving them with a collection of crisps, biscuits, chocolate and three sausage sarnies which Sketch, Matt and Mae laid claim to. Everyone sat in the living room, except for Michael who remained in the bedroom. Sketch had persuaded Clare it was ok for him to be left on his own during the meeting, but she noticed Clare was twitchy and on edge.

Before Sketch began to talk to the group about what was happening and her thoughts about what could be done Begw arrived at the flat.

"Sketch, is that a sausage you've got there? Not much left but I'll have it," she said, relieving the young woman of the remnants of her favourite meal. "What have I missed?"

"Sketch and Michael saved the Core by rebooting it because that's the answer to everything," said Trevor.

"They both came back, but Michael isn't properly with us. He's not talking," said Mae who winced at a poke in the side from Jackie.

"What Mae means is, Michael's transition wasn't as smooth as

Sketch's, and we're waiting for him to wake up. I'm sure that'll happen soon," said Jackie, smiling at Clare as she spoke.

"Oh," said Begw. "So, why are we here?" They all regarded Sketch who had positioned herself in front of the television knowing people were accustomed to gawping in its direction. She silently apologised to its energies for stealing the spotlight from them.

"We've got some news about Michael." She turned to look at Clare. "It's not going to be easy to hear."

Jackie took Clare's hand in hers in preparation for the worst.

"Michael can't be here unless he chooses to be." She surveyed the room for reactions before continuing. The faces of her friends displayed confusion.

"I was able to communicate with him using morse."

Clare got up to return to the bedroom, but Sketch stopped her. "He won't reply Clare. He's stopped communicating."

"He'll reply to me. Because...because he loves me. He loves me more..." Her words trailed off.

"More than me?" said Sketch. "That is so, but right now Michael is confused about where his loyalties lie, and it's not about you or me. It's about his duty as he sees it to the Core."

"You mean that place inside the computer?" asked Mae. "Why's he want to be there?"

"It's complicated," said Sketch.

"Oh, for God's sake," said Clare. "This isn't a game, it's not a Facebook relationship status. This is my life, his life. Don't you care?" Her face had turned a deep red and Sketch recognised anger exuding for Clare's aura. She registered her new ability to read human auras then pushed it to the side for later consideration.

"I know, and this is hard for all of us," said Sketch. "But I think there's a way to convince Michael to leave Inco behind and return to your world."

Clare's face remained rigid, but Sketch noticed a minor softening in her body language.

"Let's hear it then."

Sketch shared the details of her proposal with them. Her words were punctuated by questions, in the main from Mae who was playing catch up with the complexity of the polarised realms of existence her friend belonged to. In the end, everyone agreed to support Sketch with her scheme.

"Before we do anything, I want to spend some time with you. Just in case," she said.

"It's wise to have a just in case," said Jackie. "Maud would have had a just in case."

"I think you're right," replied Sketch.

"Who's Maud?" asked Mae, prompting a round of groans from the group.

"Matt, can we go for a walk?" asked Sketch.

He held out his hand to her. "Let's go to the heath."

Unlike the alien feeling of holding Michael's hand, the sensation of her skin touching Matt's was altogether different. Not only did it feel the most natural thing in the world, but it filled her body with a surge of life, a wave which spread throughout her creating an unstoppable smile.

"I have an unstoppable smile," she said to him as they walked through the busy streets of North London on their way to the nearest large green space in the capital.

"And it's an unstoppable smile that I love."

"You love my smile," she said with a growing grin and an urge to kiss him.

"Yes, and you know what, Sketch?"

They stopped in the middle of the pavement ignoring the rants of people trying to make their way somewhere.

"What?"

"I think...err..."

"What Matt? You think what? Just say it."

"I think I love more than just your smile."

"Oh. I love you too."

She leaned in for a kiss which equalled the first one they shared before both their worlds insisted on getting in the way. Then they continued onwards to the Heath, hand in hand, both with unstoppable smiles stuck to their faces.

"You don't have to do this, you know," said Matt as they reached a quiet section of grass and trees.

"I kind of do. If there was a way to live both ways, for all of us to be happy, then that's the choice I'd make. But none of us energies were supposed to be here. It was always supposed to be a temporary measure."

"But you changed that. You and Maud and Michael and," he laughed. "And the cat. Is the cat really from the Core?"

"There's a fair chance. A probability of about ninety-eight per cent I calculate. I'm so glad she's here. It makes your world more like home. You have no idea what it was like being the only energy alive."

"And you reckon there are more of the energies here?"

"They could be anyone, anyplace, anytime. And I can't tell who they are - look at Maud. I thought she was just a lovely old lady who was lonely and very wise."

"Everything is different now. Like how you can see our auras. You might be better at finding Core energies than before."

"True. I hope so. You understand what I've got to do though, don't you?" Sketch examined Matt's face for signs she might be making a mistake.

"Yes. Can I kiss you again?"

"You give me an unstoppable smile. You can kiss me always."

FORTY-SEVEN

London 2014

BEFORE GOING into their meeting with the Word Savers Trust, Begw made up packs with all the bid documents, budget projections and photographs for everyone pitching at the meeting. Numerous applications had been crafted by herself, Trevor and the help of Clare and sent via the ether of the Internet, with a special word from Sketch to make sure they reached their destination, to organisations offering to fund new initiatives. Some didn't bother to reply, others came with a sorry, but it wasn't a good fit for them, and a smaller number of funders suggested they liked the idea but didn't have the money to support it at this time.

Both Trevor and Begw had got to the point whereby they were ready for disappointment each time they opened an email from one of the prospective donors. When the email from the grants manager at the Word Savers Trust arrived in his inbox, Trevor didn't open it straight away. Instead, he made himself a cup of coffee and watched an episode of Tattoo Fixers, wondering once again if he should have something done to improve the one on his arm. It was only when his phone began buzzing next to his leg that he muted the sound on the TV and looked to see who was after him. He had three messages from Begw. The first said, 'Whooo hooo,' the second

'We got it,' and the third, 'Trevor, turn off the television set and go and do something less boring instead - or just read your email.'

Trevor rocketed from his prone position on the sofa to his computer where it was easier to read his email without putting on his glasses, flipped open the lid and then pumped his hand in the air. A Trust was interested in funding their save the library plan.

A considerable amount of preparation had gone into the initial application, and after the excitement at having got to the second stage, a fit of nerves took over. Trevor compensated by overeating doughnuts and Begw printed things, made packs and told everyone how they should reply to a variety of questions she'd found on an internet page about fundraising.

On the day, they gathered in the cafe area of the library, going over everything for a final time.

"Trevor," said Begw. "Pretend I'm the woman from the Word Savers Trust."

"Has she got a very straight fringe too?"

Begw's identical eyebrows lifted and her mouth pursed. "Can you not take anything seriously? This is important. IM. PORT. ANT."

"Err, sorry." Trevor, she noticed, at least had the decency to look sheepish.

"We'll try again then. Why is it that you think we should fund you and not some other deserving cause? Like donkeys or prisoners who can't read?"

"Those things are important, but people have to have some-where to go when they can read, they need places to research how to visit and help the donkeys, and they have to have somewhere they feel they belong regardless of their background," said Trevor in a more enunciated voice than he used on a day-to-day basis.

"Not bad. What's everyone else think?" Begw, looked around at Mr Moore, Clare and Rochelle from the members' committee they'd put together.

Before they could attempt an answer, the automatic doors at the front of the library slid open and through them came a young woman wearing stripy tights and multi-coloured ribbons twisted through collected strands of her hair and lips tinted with black lipstick.

"Hello, I'm looking for Begw Jones."

Begw stood and shot out her hand. "I'm Begw, Begw Jones and you are the first English person who's ever pronounced my name right the first time."

The black-lipped woman smiled, displaying brilliant white teeth with a large gap between the two in the top middle of her mouth.

"Pleased to meet you Begw. My grannie was Welsh and also called Begw. It's a grand name. I'm Lucy Taylor from the Word Savers Trust." She shook the librarian's hand before being ushered into a chair and greeting the rest of the group. Begw nodded her silent approval to Trevor.

"This is a lovely library but what will make it different to the others?" asked Lucy to the group.

"The thing is," said Mr Moore. "We're going to lend more than books and DVDs, the library will allow people to borrow other things they need but which they don't want to buy just for a one-off use." They all focused on Lucy, trying to ascertain whether she liked the idea. Begw was certain she did, or she'd not have come all the way here to meet them from south of the river.

"Can you give me some examples? Of the things you'll be lending."

"Well, last week my mum wanted to put this picture on the wall, but we don't have the drill. We used to have one, but it broke," explained Rochelle. "And dad was like, that's a lot of money just to get a picture on the wall. So, he just hammered a nail into it, bunged the art up and guess what?"

They all stared at her.

"The thing crashed down. Oh, my days and the mess. Now if we'd been able to borrow a drill, we could have done it proper. Sorry, properly."

"Ah huh," said Lucy, scribbling down notes in an A4 exercise book with dark looking unicorns on the cover. "And will there be much electrical stuff? The committee will be concerned about the health and safety risk."

"We've got that all covered," said Begw. The local electricians have agreed to test all equipment each time it comes back, and they'll do the checks for free."

Lucy cracked a smile for the first time during the questioning. They all smiled back with their most earnest happy faces.

"You seemed to have thought this through. I've just a few more questions about interest from the local community, and then I'm done."

"Really?" asked Begw. "I thought there'd be a lot more."

"Your application was very thorough. This will be plenty for me to take to our board of trustees for them to make a decision. I'll send you a memo with the details."

FORTY-EIGHT

London 2014

"TREVOR? HAVE YOU HEARD ANYTHING?" said Begw looking over his shoulder as he sat at the book checkout desk checking stock against that listed on the council's database.

"Buses, cars, some sirens, a couple talking about the failure of their relationship in the thrillers section."

"Be serious for once. I'm still your boss."

Trevor looked away from the screen and swivelled round to face Begw. "You've asked me the same thing every fifteen minutes for the last three hours. The answer is still no. Nothing from Lucy at the Word Saver's Trust about the funding."

"Oh. She seemed very efficient when we met her. I'm sure she'll be in touch soon. I could send her an email in case one of those thingies inside the computer has eaten it." Begw nudged Trevor off the office chair and plonked herself down, fingers over the keyboard in readiness to touch type her communication.

"No, don't do that. She'll think we're mad."

"Mad? What's so mad about writing an email? People do it multiple times every day."

"Begw?"

"Trevor?"

"Is there another reason why you are keen to hear from Lucy?"

"I have no idea what you are on about." She blew her fringe up with a sideways spout of air from her mouth and pushed the chair backwards. "The funding is important to us all."

"And there was me thinking you might be developing a teensy weeny crush on the woman with the stripy tights." He ducked in case Begw decided to give him a whack.

"Oh, get on with your work." She flounced off to listen in to the couple in the thrillers section.

Although she wasn't about to admit it to Trevor, she had taken a liking to Lucy, and if they got the funding, it would be like the best extra ice-cream topping to get to see her again. She rationalised with herself that her interest in the woman was in large part professional admiration, but she'd always been attracted to black lipstick. Distracted by her thoughts, she looked up to discovered she'd shelved children's classics in and amongst the novels of Stephen King. It wouldn't do to be making such rookie errors. Pull yourself together Jones, she thought. It's not as if she'd even be interested in you AND you're about to move down under for the last woman you fell in love with. Did her fancying someone else make her disloyal?

Lost in her own cloudy daydreams, Begw failed to hear Trevor call her across the library. He alerted her by shouting in her ear. "It's here. The email is here."

'It is? What does it say?"

"I don't know. I'm too scared to open it on my own."

"What does the subject line say?"

"Memo, it says bloody 'Memo'."

Taking Trevor by the arm, Begw marched to the computer. The two of them stood gazing at the screen. Begw bent down and grabbed the mouse, kicking left on the email.

Both quickly scanned it picking up the keywords the first being congratulations.

"OMG," said Trevor "We've only gone and done it." He picked up Begw and swirled her round.

"Oafff! You're banging my legs on the side of the counter."

"I don't care," said Trevor continuing to spin her around. "We got the funding!"

Begw struggled out of his grasp flung her arms around him and kissed him on the cheek.

"Hang on let's read it in detail," said Begw.

"You just want to see if Lucy gave you any kisses. Begw blushed and scowled at the same time, failing to hide her true feelings from Trevor.

"Okay. We best check to see if there are any conditions to the grant. I've heard about those online." They settle down around the computer and read through the details of the email.

"Oh," said Trevor.

"Oh indeed," said Begw. "They'll only give us the money if the council gives us the building."

"Well that puts paid to that then," said Trevor. "I can't see Winston agreeing to that. I'm sure he's hellbent on selling of the building to property developers." The exuberance and excitement of the last few minutes disappeared into the air. Their expressions were tinged with tiredness, their smiles turned to frowns.

"Is it down to Winston though? I'm sure the final decision doesn't rest with him. The council, the councillors have to decide on the big stuff. There's bound to be a committee that deals with buildings, premises, property et cetera."

"Oh yeah," said Trevor "That's the truth. Get on the Google and let's find out who they are."

It took a little searching to find a list of members of the property allocation committee at the local council although it was hidden away in the back of the website as it was something scandalous.

"That's a list of names, and I don't recognise anyone on it," said Begw.

"Who do you think is the most important?" asked Trevor running his finger up and down the screen.

"Well that chap at the top, David Lloyd is the Chair. We should try him first. Jot down his email address and let's send him a giant memo."

"You and your memos," sighed Trevor, but his face was filled with mischief and there was a sparkle in his eye.

Between them they constructed a message outlining their plan and the public support for it, and sent it off to the councillor in charge of the committee. Attached was their funding application and the offer from the Word Savers Trust.

"Not much more we can do now," said Trevor. "But you should reply to Lucy and acknowledge the offer. You might even suggest meeting up to discuss the condition of the building."

"Ummm," said Begw. "It would be rude not to."

Trevor chuckled to himself as he ambled off to talk to some people looking confused about how to login to the library computer network.

Begw twisted her lips around and focused on her reply.

FORTY-NINE

London 2014

____

"THE THING I don't get. Well there are lots of things I don't get," said Mae, sucking a blue smoothie which matched her hair, through a metal straw. "But the big thing I don't get is how you can live without a body."

Sketch laughed. "It would be impossible to fit inside the computer if we had physical forms."

"I think I'll keep imagining lots of little people in there, busying away, making things work and let's face it, it's great having something to blame when I do something wrong."

"Mae! That's not fair."

"I know, but it's funny right?" She pushed her smoothie across the table of the cafe. "Here, try some of this. Bet you like it more than that yucky espresso you've taken to drinking. I blame Harry. Talking of which, have you heard from him?"

Sketch took a moment to slurp up some of the blue drink. "Nice, full of sugar but then you need a bit of something sweet now and then." She wiped the remains of the liquid from around her lips, marvelling at how it could have got there when she was using a straw. "Not a sausage. I love how people say that. Not much is a sausage is apart from a sausage."

"You are so weird!"

"And now you know why," said Sketch returning to her coffee.

"Guess what?"

"No. Tell me."

"I'm so never going to do drugs, because life, this life is like a great big hallucination. You going to say something to Harry then?"

Looking at her friend, Sketch wondered if that was an option. "Don't think so. There's no point. And there is plenty of other fish in the sea. See, I'm getting super good at all these linguistic quirks and sayings."

"When you say fish, are you talking about someone close by beginning with M."

Sketch scouted around with her eyes as if trying to locate something. "I don't "I spy" anyone here except you and me." She laughed.

"Oh, you can be so annoying. I mean Matt. Not my type but I guess he's ok. And I saw the way you looked at him when you guys went off the other day."

Sketch hid her face in her hand and then peeped out between her fingers, her mouth stuck in an unstoppable smile.

"Ooooh, I'm right," said Mae.

"Yes, it's a thing."

"And can you kiss and stuff with you being an alien and all that?"

The mouthful of Americano Sketch had just taken splurted out of her mouth, down her chin and into the table. "I'm not an alien!"

"You know what I mean. In fact, just tell me again what you are. The whole business is messing with my head."

"Right now, I'm a human, the same as you, but before I lived in a place called the Core."

"And that's the inside of the computer?"

"Yes, the Core exists to serve human users, and it is made up of energies who make things happen. Things like when you click on a website link, move the cursor across the screen."

"That's mad! You do stuff like that. My mind is properly blown."

"But Jackie told you everything already."

"But you saying it just made shit real. Sorry, my grandma is always saying I swear too much, but you get me, right?"

Sketch fiddled with the zip on her jacket pocket until it opened. She took out her phone. "Selfie time?"

"Go on then, though you looked heaps better with the coloured hair."

"When I transferred back from the Core, I reset myself. Technically I'm born again."

They positioned themselves behind the smartphone adjusting the heads, smiles and pouts til they reached the optimum picture position and took multiple snaps.

"Sketch? Would you be able to do something for me?"

"Sure. Well, I think I will, but I can't be one hundred per cent sure until you tell me what it is."

"Ha!" Mae stuck her tongue out. "It's about my Grandma. You know she was mates with your oldie friend Maud?" Sketch nodded. "Well, she keeps going on about you. She's not well. Might have to go into a home and that's not right, but there's not much anyone can do."

Sketch squeezed Mae's arm. "How can I help?"

"She won't believe me that I gave you that letter. Doesn't matter what I say it doesn't stop her. Will you come and tell her yourself?"

"Mae, I'd love to meet your grandma. Maybe she can tell me more about Maud's life. What it was like for her being here."

"She can talk about the old days for hours, literally hours. Not so good on yesterday and what my name is but great on the past."

"Let's go this afternoon," said Sketch coming alive at the idea of meeting someone who'd known Maud for so long. She shoved her phone back into the pocket of her jacket and picked up both of their cups to deposit on the counter on the way out.

"Ok, but she'll be having a nap right now, so if we head over there, we'll have to hang out in Tottenham for a while."

"Cool," said Sketch. "I've never been out that way. Bus or tube?"

"Northern line to Euston and then Victoria to Seven Sisters, or we could get a bus to Finsbury Park and pick up the underground there."

"Let's take the tube. I love the tube. It's a miracle."

Mae arose and went in for a high five as Sketch moved away with the cups and collided with her friend. The crockery flew into the air and then tumbled down to the floor and into pieces.

"Whoops!" said Mae.

FIFTY

London 2014

ARMED WITH WEDGES OF PAPER, diagrams, PowerPoint presentations, laptops and all the statistics they could muster, Begw set off to wage war with the council premises committee and her arch nemesis Winston. She had arranged to meet Lucy the funder, in a coffee shop next to the council offices for a pre-battle pow-wow about strategy, so left the library an hour and a half early. She didn't want to be late and make a bad impression with the beautiful woman. Every time she thought things like this, she berated herself for being disloyal to Deborah, but she reminded herself there was no harm in admiring someone for their all-round loveliness. Once she was in Sydney and starting her new life, she'd banish all thoughts of Lucy. She wouldn't need them to make her smile because she'd be where she was supposed to be. But having remembered where her affections were supposed to lie, she put on her serious, professional librarian face before arriving at the cafe.

"Hey, Begw. How lovely to see you," said Lucy, giving her a hug and putting the happy beam back onto Begw's face and making her forget all her good intentions.

"You too. Shall we have a coffee?" asked Begw.

"I think that kind of fuel is exactly what we need at this point in time. I'll get them, and then we can run through our pitch. Don't look so worried my Welsh friend, we funders have a lot of sway and I will do my utmost to make sure your library isn't shut down for good."

Begw attempted to bring her mind back to the matter at hand, the meeting with the council, but Lucy's words had taken over her mind. *She called me her Welsh friend*, thought Begw. *Friend, just a friend, or does she call all her grantees friends?* She picked the camera function on her phone reversing the picture so she could see herself in the screen display double checking that she hadn't put on too much blusher or that she wasn't in fact blushing. As Lucy returned, she pretended to be scrawling through her emails, trying to look professional.

"They never stop, do they? Emails," said Lucy. She sat down opposite Begw and commenced giving her a pep talk.

"I'm sure you know all this already, but I think it's important always to say it just to remind ourselves. One, if you look confident and sound confident the people you're talking to will believe it. If you get stuck when you're talking, look at me, and I'll chip in with some of my snazzy finder stuff. Two, the council love nothing more than anything to be seen to be working in partnership with not for profits, especially if the money is coming from elsewhere. It would be terrible press for them to say no to our request."

"You make it sound effortless," said Begw. "If it's that easy why haven't they said yes already?"

"Ah, that's the thing. They love the due process. That's what they'll tell you anyway, but really I think they just like people to jump through lots and lots of hoops."

"Well, that fits with the dealings I've had with them over the years. A lot of talk, a lot of paperwork and not a lot of action except when it comes to cutting services."

"I suppose the financial situation isn't all their fault. A lot of the cuts comes from central government."

They ran through the key points they wanted to make to the council in their presentation.

"Goodness, is that the time? We best get ourselves in there," said Lucy gathering together the collection of materials from the table.

Because the council office where the meeting was to take place was close to the coffee shop, they had no problem reaching reception, registering and making their way to the room in the corner of the open-plan office. It was the same space the libraries team occupied along with various other departments in the council. Begw knew it well from visits to her boss Winston over the years, including the time he had had her unfairly suspended and the subsequent meeting when the disciplinary action was overturned and she was reinstated to her post as librarian. She chuckled as she brought to mind the look on his face when he'd been overruled by the HR panel.

"You sound jollier," said Lucy.

"That's because I've remembered who we're up against and I know all the ways to get under his skin and make him sweat his way through the meeting."

Lucy slowed down and gestured at Begw to do the same. "We have to look professional."

"Oh, don't worry. I'm an expert at that. No one except Winston and I will have a clue what's going on."

"Are you sure?"

"I swear on the honour of Tom Jones," said Begw with a straight face.

A tinkle of the dirtiest laugher Begw had ever heard came from Lucy's mouth leaving her edging towards a full-on crush.

"Let's do this thing," said Begw leading the way to the room.

Her knock on the door was answered by Marilyn, Winston's long-term and hard done by assistant who beckoned them in and winked at Begw, mouthing the words 'good luck' when she was faced away from the officials in the room.

Around a rectangular table with a spider phone for teleconferencing in a central position were three white, overweight men with receding hairlines. Two of them Begw knew well, and the other was a councillor whose name she'd only read on the council website and paperwork circulated about their proposal.

"Hello Begw," said the man opposite. "And you must be Lucy. I'm Justin Tiverton." He extended his right hand to her.

"Pleased to meet you. It's great to have the opportunity to talk to you about this exciting community project. It ticks so many boxes for us as a funder."

She smiled at the three men one by one, yet again impressing Begw with her approach.

A round of introductions confirmed the other two men in the room were Winston and Henry Taylor. Begw worked hard not to show her nerves and act in the way that made Winston believe she was brimming with confidence and in control. However, she wasn't doing the best job of convincing herself this was the case.

Justin as head of the panel led the conversation. "We've had some time to consider this proposal of yours Begw, and it does have some merits. You'll be aware, for quite some time the council has been struggling to balance the books - no pun intended - with all the cuts coming from central government, and while we're all keen to protect library facilities for the public it's difficult to defend them when social services for older people children and young people are being slashed."

Begw had heard these arguments before, and Trevor had warned her it was likely they would be used at the meeting as advised by his online library warrior friends around the country.

Justin continued the speech Begw assumed was preparatory. "We don't have the resources to support what you're proposing."

"But we have the funding," said Begw glancing at Lucy sitting next to her. "What we need now is the space. Surely that's in your gift."

"Yes," said Lucy. " The Trust has committed to providing costs for staffing, setting up the new organisation, providing the basic resources and support for volunteers for the next three years. But we do require the commitment of the council as a partner." She looked at the trio of men with a serious expression fixed on her face that said don't mess with me.

Justin glanced at Henry.

"The council needs all its property. Including the building the library is currently housed in." What was enraging Begw was the way the three men appeared not to be listening to what they had to say. They walked into the room having already decided what the outcome of the discussion was going to be.

"What is it you want it for?" She said. There's a rumour going around that developers have got their eyes on it. It would make a lot of money for the council if you turned into flats. And we all know dosh is something short you're of."

"That's just like you Begw," said Winston sitting upright in his chair, so his large stomach bulged onto the table. "Making stuff up. This isn't the first time you've come up with a load of lies. Like when you rounded up all those old people and told them, we were closing down the library."

Begw managed the biggest sigh she could pull from her body and rolled it in his direction in an overly dramatic manner. "But you were closing down the library," she said.

Henry and Justin looked at each other and then at Winston.

"Miss Jones is right on this occasion Winston," said Henry Taylor. "We should get back to the matter at hand. There is no intention or commitment or agreement from the council to do anything with the building the local library is in. However," he said to Begw and Lucy. "It is a building that we own and can raise substantial revenue from to support other services, services which the local community is screaming out for."

Both Lucy and Begw started to talk at the same time, Lucy's words just pipping Begw's to the post. "We at the trust commend the commitment to the community that the council has. And libraries play many functions for people living in a local area as I'm sure you're aware. They're not merely there as a lending facility, they play a vital social role in bringing people together, creating cohesive environments where people feel safe and feel they belong."

Begw decided this was the time to use the ace up her sleeve when it came to Winston. From her bag, she pulled out a cardboard folder imprinted with the words, 'Begw Jones and her library rebels'. She slid it into sight of Winston, tapping her fingers to attract his attention. She'd been given the collection of documents from

Winston's PA Marilyn in a secret meeting they'd had a week ago after Marilyn approached her offering to help. The PA told her Winston had been spying on Begw and her friends. The folder contains multiple incriminating documents covered with scribbled notes where Winston recorded his plans to plot the downfall of anyone who got in the way of his retirement plans. From across the table, she saw him recognise the folder and the blood drained from his face. As panic took over sweat began to appear in droplets on his forehead, and he loosened his tie and collar. "Are you alright Winston?" asked Justin. "We can take a break if you need some air." Winston coughed. "No, no carry on. I just need some water. Begw being closest to a jug of water and glasses poured him a drink and handed it to him.

"Winston," she said. "You've been involved with the libraries in this area for many years and as such you be able to attest to how important they are for the local people." Begw smiled and was relishing the discomfort she saw Winston experiencing.

"Well yes, people do seem to like the library."

"It still comes down to the building," said Lucy. "This is a brilliant plan. You have no idea how many proposals drop through our letterbox every day or how many emails we get asking for support. This is one of the best ones I've seen ever. It will be a terrible shame for it to all fail before it begins because the local council couldn't find it within themselves to provide some space, don't you think?"

"We wouldn't be able to give you the space for free, you understand," said Justin. "But there might be a way we can do a deal which makes the rent affordable for a period of time."

"Might that be for a period of three years?" Said Lucy.

"I'll have to consult with my colleagues," suggesting he looked at Henry for a nod of assent. "But it's something we could consider."

Begw threw Winston her best victory grin and experienced a surge of energy run through her body as Lucy grabbed her hand under the table.

FIFTY-ONE

London 2014

IT WAS the first time Sketch had travelled to Tottenham although she'd read a lot about the area on the Internet and the news. The diverse area had a bad rep and suffered from being stuck with the negative associations of riots and unrest, but Sketch figured if her Mae was okay with it then it was fine. Her friend wasn't going to take her somewhere dangerous. As they got off the tube at Seven Sisters station, she thought the surrounding area was much like other bits of London she'd seen, full of lots of different types of shops and varying kinds of people weaving in and out and along the pavements, alongside an array of vehicles.

"Just down this way, about ten minutes' walk," said Mae pointing in the direction of the High Road heading north. You don't mind walking, do you? We could get the bus."

"Walking is great," said Sketch. "I like taking in the air around me, even if it isn't fresh."

Sketch and Mae trundled along the path avoiding people coming in the opposite direction and the occasional bicycle which strayed onto the pavement. They turned off the High Road onto a street which was home to a small block of flats where Beverley Mae's grandma lived. From the outside, they appeared unkempt, the walls in need of a lick of paint and some weeds growing up from the cracks between the paving stones.

"It's up this way," said Mae, leading Sketch up a concrete stairway to the side of the central section of the building. The space lacked adequate lighting and made Sketch wonder what it must be like to come home here alone in the dark. She shivered.

"Grandma's flat is on the second floor. There is a lift, but most of the time it's broken. I'm not risking us getting stuck between floors. There was this man who lived here who got stuck for two days. Was near death when they got him out."

Sketch suppressed a giggle not knowing if Mae's story was true or the product of one of her melodramatic moments when she embellished the facts. Beverley's door was clean and marked by a large ceramic pot with rosemary, thyme and mint growing in different sections.

"I did that," said Mae. "Had to get something out of those gardening lessons." She turned the key in the Yale lock and turned on the light in the small hall as they entered.

"Hey Grandma, it's your favourite granddaughter."

"Violet?" Beverley's voice floated through from behind the living room door. Mae tutted and turned to Sketch. "It's her memory. Violet is my crazy cousin, but I'm defo her favourite. She likes my hair."

"Because it's blue?" asked Sketch.

"Who's there?" said Beverley. Mae pushed open the living room door and bounced in and gave the old woman a hug. "Just me, Grandma. Me and Sketch this is." The confusion left Beverley's eyes, and a smile grew across the breadth of her face.

"Sketch."

"Yes, Grandma. You kept asking for her."

The woman looked Sketch up and down making her squirm. "Come over and sit next to me girl." Sketch glanced at Mae for verification, and when her friend nodded, she moved across the room to a brown armchair identical to the one Beverley sat on.

"Hello," she said. "I'm Sketch, you knew my friend Maud."

Beverley took Sketch's hand and clasped it between hers. "My dear. I have a letter for you."

"No, Grandma. You gave me the letter to give to Sketch."

"Did I?"

Sketch pulled the yellowed envelope from her packet. "Here it is. I've got it. It was so kind of you to keep it for me all these years. Maud would be so pleased to know I got it."

"You got the letter?"

"I have the letter, and I've read it more than once. Here it is." She removed her hand from Beverley's and replaced it with the letter. The older woman smiled.

"You got the letter. She wanted you to have it. Made me promise that no matter what I gave you the letter."

"What was she like when she was younger?"

"When I met her, she was strong, direct and feisty, but kind and her kindness, it grew for each year she lived. She was a remarkable woman, but she wasn't of this world."

"What do you mean Grandma?" asked Mae looking at Sketch.

"So kind, so special and she always seemed ready for what was coming. Kind of like she could see the future. I once asked her if she could read the tea leaves." Mae and Sketch sat mouths open waiting for the next bit of the sentence.

"Come on Grandma. Tell us what Maud said."

Beverley scowled at her Granddaughter. "You younger generation don't have no manners or patience. I'm thinking."

Eyebrows raised but neither of the young women said another word while they waited for Beverley to continue.

"She laughed. Didn't say nothing but I knew she was something special. So special." She switched her attention back to Sketch. "She told me if for any reason I lost the letter to make sure to tell you this. Don't go back because it's not there anymore. But I didn't lose the letter."

"No, you didn't."

"You promise. You promise not to go back like Maud said?"

There wasn't an answer Sketch wanted to give. One would be a lie, the other would hurt Beverley. She couldn't promise and had not yet decided the best option. Weighing it up in her mind Sketch reasoned that Maud hadn't had all the information when she wrote the letter. She didn't know what happened after the initial evacuation of the Core or why it had become vital for someone to take on the role of the One, but Sketch had learnt enough from humans and their fractured and often brutal history to know that a vacuum could result in the worst of circumstances. This didn't make it any easier to tell Beverley the truth so, recalling a conversation with Maud about how sometimes telling a lie for the sake of kindness was ok.

"I promise," she said.

FIFTY-TWO

London2014

WHEN SKETCH first met Trevor in the library, she'd not been sure what to make of him. He'd asked her about boys and foisted Story Time off on her because it wasn't his favourite thing to do. On the whole, he'd been kind, but she hadn't had many humans to compare him with. However, he'd turned out to be a loyal, generous and fun-loving friend, not only to her but to others around him. Meeting him before she travelled back to the Core left her with mixed emotions. She missed being his flatmate.

"I wish you could come with me," she said.

"Watching TV has never been the same without you," replied Trevor over a pint of beer in the Tufnell Park Tavern, where they'd ended up because there was nowhere to sit in The Pineapple. The vibe in the pub reflected the clientele, many of whom came for the gastro food and candles as much as they did for the beer, wine and spirits. Sketch enjoyed it and had a passion for their rosemary coated triple cooked chips. They were perfectly combined with lashing of the spicy tomato sauce the pub made themselves.

Trevor played with his beer mat before flicking it across the table aiming it at Sketch.

"Are you sure we'll be able to talk this time?" he asked.

"Unless something I've not anticipated goes wrong. So, when I'm free, we can hook up and watch 'Tattoos for Geeks' and 'The Batchelor'. Make sure the screen is facing the TV, or I won't be able to see anything. Oh, and the mic needs to be active on the computer too. Imagine how awful it would be if I missed the finding out who that annoying rich bloke chooses to be his wife."

Trevor faked a horrified look and then raised his pint glass to cheers Sketch.

"You do that a lot," she said, returning the gesture with a clink.

"Probably cos I drink too much."

Sketch didn't disagree. He did drink too much, but she wasn't one to judge.

"Where's Begw?"

"She messaged to say she'll be over in a bit. Says she's got some news for us," said Trevor.

"Ohhhh, whatever could that be?"

"Well..."

"Well, what? You know something. Tell me, Trevor!" Sketch loved human gossip when it was good news and something about Trevor's demeanour lead her to believe there was nothing to worry about. "Is it about her moving to Australia?"

"Can't tell you."

"Oh, go on. I'm about to burst with not knowing."

Trevor snorted. "I couldn't count on two hands the number of times you've nearly burst with not knowing."

"Humans and energies don't burst," she laughed. "You should know that by now. Oh, there you are Begw."

The Welsh librarian approached their table with three glasses and a bottle of fizzy wine.

"Hello. Budge up and make room for them."

"The fringe is looking good," said Sketch.

"Why thank you, Sketch. I always knew you'd learn to appreciate the beauty of a straight fringe. Not everyone has the forehead for it, you know."

Begw proceeded to open the bottle of Prosecco as getting the top off bottles of fizz was one of her specialities to the point that she'd considered listing it on her CV. She poured them each a glass and handed them around.

"There you go Sketch. IECHYD DA." More clinking of glasses took place between them.

"What are we celebrating, Begw?" asked Sketch, not caring as long as she got to drink the fizzy stuff.

"Two things. The first is we got the funding for the library, AND the council have signed an agreement saying we can have rent the space for three hundred pounds a month."

"That's amazing! What made them cave and go so low on the rent?" asked Sketch who was overcome with joy that the library would be safe from closure, at least for the next three years.

"Begw convinced them," said Trevor.

"I'd love to take credit for it, given my superior ability to make a convincing argument, but it was down to Lucy from the funders. She did some grant giver magic on them, and they backed down."

"Tell her about Winston," said Trevor waving around another beermat.

" Oh yeah, that's another exciting bit," said Begw. "As a result of his incompetence and someone, I can't say who, leaking a file containing his own self-reported misdemeanours over the years and his weirdo stalking of people to his superiors he's been given the sack."

"No!" said Sketch. "A bit of me feels a bit sorry for him." Trevor and Begw looked at her with their mouth open.

"The flies will get in," she said to them. "I'm just joking. He's brought it on himself. And with the money they'll save from his salary they can help some of the people in the community who need support."

"Well said Sketch," said Begw. "Now all I need to work out is where I'm gonna get my sausages from without stealing them from you."

"Won't they have sausages in Australia?"

"I dunno. And that leads me to the second thing we got to celebrate." Trevor's lips turned down at the corners as if to frown.

"There's not much to celebrate about you leaving us to go and live thousands of miles away in the sunshine with us in London here in the cold and the rain for most of the year."

Sketch spotted a twinkle in Begw's eyes although her face remained straight serious as was the norm for the librarian.

"I'm not going," she said.

"Suppose I can save up and come for my holidays though," said Trevor.

Begw snorted, and Sketch giggled. Both of them clinked glasses and winked.

"I think you should get your ears tested Trevor. You're not working for me otherwise."

You what?" Said Trevor. "Did you just say you're not going?"

"Lucy's offered me a job managing the library project for the trust."

"No!" Said Trevor sporting a wide-mouthed frog sized grin. "I'm never gonna get rid of you."

" I think we're going to need another bottle of champagne," said Begw. "I'm not going near that bar again though. Sketch, take my bank card and go for me."

FIFTY-THREE

London 2014

———————————

THE SOFA SAT where it always sat, adjacent to the window in the basement of the Townsend's townhouse. Sitting with Jackie, Sketch realised a circle was being created and that circles never end. Because of this, the conversation she was about to have was not finite, and new exciting pathways would spring from it.

Jackie knew what was coming. She had prepared herself for such an eventuality, and there was a big box of tissues on the arm of the sofa for nose blowing, the wiping away of tears and if deemed necessary for white flag waving. The box was labelled man-sized, a concept Sketch and Jackie had spoken about previously. Sketch found it bizarre to call tissues nowhere near the approximated the size of a human man by such a name, and where was the women's size box of tissues? Both agreed it was ludicrous but that the tissues still did perform their purpose in wiping away bodily fluids and makeup. Jackie pulled two such tissues from the box and handed one to Sketch, keeping the other for herself.

"I'm a little lost for words Sketch," said Jackie. "Life, my life and those of all the people around you have been transformed. It's not the same as it was."

211

"Nothing stays still. If it weren't me there would have been something else to make a change in your life."

"True, but it wouldn't have been half as much fun! All the swirling, all the smiles and seeing the world through your eyes."

Sketch stood up, took Jackie's hand and pulled her from the squidgy sofa.

"Come on."

Jackie laughed and allowed herself to be dragged to an upright position.

"Let's swirl and dance. There's no music so let's pretend like we're at one of those secret discos."

"Silent discos you mean?"

Sketch grinned a grin which bounced across her face. "That's the one. Still not getting it all right."

"That's the human part of you."

The two women danced it out in the small spaces in the basement family room, bouncing, jiggling, shaking their heads, hair and random body parts and spinning until dizziness took over after which they collapsed laughing on the sofa. It took a minute for Jackie to catch her breath.

"Wow, I'd forgotten how much fun jumping up and down was. Like being a kid again or the days when we used to go clubbing through the night."

"I know," replied Sketch hugging a cushion with a skinny giraffe printed onto its front. "Everything has been mega intense like life had too much coffee and got a bit hyper and out of control. Being able to sparkle and spin always makes it better."

She adjusted herself to an upright sitting position. "Make sure you keep sparkling and spinning."

Jackie nodded and stroked her thumb across Sketch's cheek. "Will I see you again?"

"Yes, of course, you will. There'll be no stopping me. Let me get things sorted, and then everything will be more fluid." Sketch could see Jackie didn't understand what she meant. Being between two worlds affected the language she used. She went from a little bit London to a little bit the Core and even confused herself at times. "I have to make things right in the Core, then I can come back, but Jackie, I've got a proposition for you."

"You do?"

"Don't look so scared. I think you're going to like this one."

"Go on then, tell me what it is."

In the space of the next few minutes, Sketch shared her idea with Jackie, stopping now and then to answer questions from her friend.

"Wow," said Jackie. "I'm blown away. So, you can take me from my body and turn me into an energy inside the computer."

"Yes, you'll be part of the Core, see what it's like on our side. I had a lot of time to think about it when I was trapped there. It's daft that the process only goes one way. After all, if you are to be a liaison between your world and mine you need to understand it from both sides."

"It makes sense. It makes total sense, but you're wrong about it not being scary. It could go wrong, and I might get stuck there or worse."

"Or you could have the biggest adventure a human has ever had. Plus, it will make a huge difference in our efforts to track down the missing energies who were dispersed to the physical plane of the earth."

They stopped talking and imagined what once might have sounded like science fiction.

"It's good to remember those who have made this possible for us. Like Virder and Maud, but it's time to look forward and take the best bits of both worlds and make something resembling an enormous smile of a world," said Sketch. "Let's make it all shine."

She high-fived Jackie. "It's weird though. The emotions I thought were human ones, like sadness, excitement, happiness, I think I had them in the Core too. Energies, our kind of energies aren't supposed to feel things, we're meant to be neutral."

"Reckon there still might be a lot of stuff about the universe that even you clever energies haven't worked out yet."

"And a smidgen of mystery makes life that bit more exciting, right?" asked Sketch as she watched Jackie's aura grow bolder and brighter.

"Wouldn't be without it. Just think how boring everything would be."

The clock ticked time by as the sun fell out of the sky. "That's it then," said Jackie.

"For now. Let's get everyone else here. It wouldn't be the same without them."

FIFTY-FOUR

The Core

THIS TIME, Sketch's return to the Core provided fewer unexpected challenges. The environment remained as she had left it, except for the negative pulses of light which had represented the former dictatorship of the One. It gave her positive buzz to have the freedom to release the potential of her nature as an energy. Her aura lit up as bright as it was possible for it to rise to and she spun around firing out sparks of light that twisted as they travelled through the space around her. This time being back in the Core was fantastic.

Despite her enthusiasm about being on home turf, Sketch reined in an element of her excitement, knowing there were still serious conversations to be had and that Inco hadn't had warning of her transformation back to the Core. She couldn't predict how he would react but had made the decision based upon her thinking that he'd be more likely to listen to what she had to propose if there'd been no time to examine the idea beforehand.

She squeezed in another burst of firework-like displays of happiness before calling out to him in pulses across the expanse of the Core. When Inco acknowledged her message, Sketch, moved through the space as if she'd never inhabited a human body, revealing in the sensation of having no physical form to constrain her. This was one of the major advantages of being a computer energy. They came together in an area empty of other energies.

"Sketch, you are unexpected in the Core."

"And there was me thinking you'd be lighting up at the thought of me being here with you," she said, approximating a wink of an eye using her aura. It was a trick she'd been hoping to affect on her return. "Oh, did you see what I did then? Super cool use of the energy."

"You came here to play tricks with the life force of the Core?"

Sketch moderated her behaviour and her aura adjusted to match.

"No, I came here to talk."

"How is Clare?"

"Kind of how you'd expect, but she's bearing up. Mae has agreed to do some shifts with her at Urban Rootz, so she's keeping busy."

"Things here remain fragile. The new intake is inexperienced. You may have freezes and glitches with the system." said Inco. It struck Sketch how professional his pulses were. They failed to give away the extent of their previous friendship.

"Trevor's not said much to that effect, but then he's aware things might not be as smooth as they should for a period. How have you been?"

Inco didn't respond, but Sketch saw a ripple run through his aura indicating he was searching for an appropriate response. She waited, preparing her next set of pulses.

"I am kind of how you'd expect, but bearing up," said Inco.

"It doesn't have to be like this, you know?"

"The Core needs stability. It is why we exist."

Sketch knew her friend had been changed by his experience as a human, by living by their ways, rules and with their emotional, hormonal makeup. "Yes, but it doesn't have to be you that makes sure that it is."

"There's no one else. All the other energies here are newly transformed. They require training, and very few of them have had previous experiences which allow them to be fast-tracked to key positions of responsibility. On the whole, they have the level of aptitude you do."

Sketch sparkled. "Oh, Inco. That is a challenge, but it still doesn't mean it's you who has to do it. Not on your own anyway."

They examined each others' auras. Sketch willed him to realise what she was talking about, thinking she couldn't make it any more obvious than it already was. His thinking aura remained in play for longer than her patience.

"You're not the only energy who has experience. There's another one, and they are in your immediate proximity." Getting still no response of comprehension she went one stage further. "As Ashling would say, you are such a dufus sometimes. I am the other energy. I can stay here and lead the Core so you can return to Clare in the human world."

"No, no. That can't happen." He fronted her, energy to energy in a way that once would have put her on edge, but Sketch knew Inco well, knew how people and energies put up barriers because they were afraid for themselves or for others and often scared of making big, existence-changing decisions.

She pushed massaging, calming light towards him. "It can," she said without any tone to her pulse, hoping her neutrality might convince him of the serious nature of her proposal. "You love Clare. She loves you, and you've lived more of your life as a human than I have."

"But you have your human family to consider."

"I've talked it through with them. They understand why this is necessary. But please hear me out because I think we both have an important part to play in this and there's a way it can be mutually beneficial."

Inco's reluctance was still evident, but Sketch was reassured by the temperance of his aura and that he'd stopped jolting around as if agitated.

"Out there in the human world are no end of displaced energies. We don't know if they are aware of their situation, if they remember their previous life in the Core or if they are struggling to live a life in a world, they weren't prepared to be catapulted into. Agreed?"

Inco pulsed his affirmation of her statements.

"Clare told me how important you thought it was to track them down and offer them support and solace, and I happen to think you are right. Look at what you went through when you transformed."

"So, you plan to find them all?" he asked.

"Not me. I think you should be the one to do it. And Clare wants to help you find them." Unable to contain her excitement at her amazing plan, even though she'd not finished sharing it with Inco, Sketch began to spin and spin and spin until he joined her. They spiralled around vacant areas of the Core until they reached the human observation platform.

"Look," pulsed Sketch. "They are all there." On the other side of the monitor's screen were assembled Ashling, Sammy, Matt, Clare, Trevor, Begw and Jackie and some woman with black lipstick who Sketch didn't recognise.

"I promised we'd communicate with them, so they know we're both safe. Not like before when I returned, and they and you heard nothing but silence from this side of the world."

Sketch wasn't sure if Inco was taking in her pulses, but she could see his aura flowing in the direction of Clare who stood in the centre of the group of friends. And his aura glowed with radiance and warmth.

"We're rigged up to the device that the former the One gave Jackie, the One who became Maud," Sketch said. "Let's call her Maud from now on. It will be less confusing for everyone."

"And we can call the last the One, the Tyrant," replied Inco with an aura reminiscent of when she first encountered him.

"Done. Let's do some pulsing and morsing to all those lovely people out there. Oh, I do love them so."

"And the boy Matt?" asked Inco.

"I love him the best."

They put the protocols in place within the Core to activate the human device and commence communications. It allowed them to send and receive messages by text.

- Hello, this is Sketch and Inco (Michael) checking in with the human world.

-OMG, you are ok!

Trevor was designated the typist for the group chat.

- We're both fine. I'm going to hand over to Inco now.

At the same time, Trevor swapped places with Clare so she could talk through keystrokes to Inco.

-Hello, my love.

-Hello Clare. It's optimal to see your face. You look well.

-Has Sketch told you the plan?

Inco turned to Sketch. "Not all of it," she said. "Tell them I am going to after we've all spoken." He repeated her words to Clare and the others and watched as they exchanged glances with one another and looked back at him with anxious smiles.

-Michael. Whatever you decide, it's alright with me. As long as we can speak, and this proves it's possible.

Her face held a hopeful smile that shone through her eyes as well as her lips.

-Sketch, everyone here says they love you.

As the words appeared as text in the Core, all the humans held up banners with the words 'We love you Sketch.' She filled with an awesome spirit of love which made her aura soar higher than she could have imagined being possible. Taking the controls back from Inco, she sent her response.

-And I love you too. Oh, what beautiful humans you are. I'm sending a kiss and a hug. And Matt, an extra one for you. Be strong.

They all waved and as planned shut down their end of the communications link.

The joint brightness of Sketch and Inco's auras lit up the Core, and she could see the new recruits who populated its expanse watching their joy.

"Inco, we're being observed."

"Yes, we should moderate our auras to set an appropriate standard of behaviour, but let's pause for a moment and enjoy the feeling of freedom."

When they came to tone down their mood, they did it in gradients, in sync with each other.

"Your plan, Sketch. It's time you told me what it is."

"You know some of it. I will stay while you return to the human world to seek out the displaced energies. That leaves me to stay here in the Core and lead the energies."

"As the One."

"Yes. I hope I can perform the role in the way it should be done, but I have had two role models who demonstrated well, what how it should be and what not to do."

"I'm still not convinced it is wise for you to give up your human side. You took to it so much better than I did."

"But that's the beauty of my plan. As you locate the missing energies, those who choose can return and begin to take control and lead alongside me. This will leave me free to spend time in the human world. There's no reason to have to decide between one place or the other when I can have both."

"Is that not greedy?" said Inco, his aura giving away his excitement where his words did not.

"No, it's perfect," said Sketch migrating into another light spiral. "Oh, and the first energy you will find living with Jackie. She's a cat, and she's pretty special. Send her back to me as soon as you can and then get busy finding the others."

Stay in touch - join my mailing list

Acknowledgments

Writing a series of books has been like jumping on a plane blind-folded with no idea where you will land. On the whole, it's been a blast and sometimes I've landed on white beaches with accompanying turquoise seas. Not only have I created a world of imaginary friends but I've been motivated by the amazing people I know and love in the human world.

My inner circle Your World team is make up of remarkable humans. Special hugs and thanks to Laura Goodman, Hayley Reed and Melanie Kearney for being the most eager beta readers ever, to Adam (Ads) Wilsher for editing and putting up with my not so subtle 'are you finished yet?' emails and texts, to Cerian Lloyd Jones for her unerring belief in Memos and all things North Waleian and to Jennie Rawlings for yet another beautiful cover design which makes me smile. I'm privileged to have you all as part of my team.

Thanks to my family who are stuck with me ('Hey, Nigel and Puffin, love Auntie Josh).

A giant sized thanks to my second family - the one I chose for myself. For being there when I talk rubbish and convince you to do things you would otherwise think better of, for mopping up my tears when emotions overtake me and telling me when to most definitely swipe left.

This list is not exclusive but some people deserve a special mention: Rachel, Matt and all at Craving Coffee for providing the best coffee ever and allowing me to demand off menu cocktails, James and Laura for introducing me to the idea of a library of things and generally being amazing, Martine for being my biggest fan, the Women in Tottenham massive, the incredible people I work with, all of you who have introduced me to exciting new things and new people, and to Solly for making me smile in the way only a 3 year old can.

Thank you to everyone who has read my books - it's a joy to share the worlds in my mind with you. And remember when your IT is playing up - there's a reason for it.

About the Author

Anj Cairns lives in North London, loves all things book, reading, writing, food and coffee.

Follow, like, contact, love
www.anjcairns.com
anj@anjcairns.com